# THE BRIDE BOX

# THE BRIDE BOX

## Michael Pearce

This first world edition published 2013
in Great Britain and the USA by
SEVERN HOUSE PUBLISHERS LTD of
19 Cedar Road, Sutton, Surrey, England, SM2 5DA.

British Library Cataloguing in Publication Data

Pearce, Michael, 1933-
    The bride box. – (A Mamur Zapt mystery ; 17)
    1. Owen, Gareth Cadwallader (Fictitious character)–
    Fiction. 2. Egypt–History–British occupation,
    1882-1936–Fiction. 3. Detective and mystery stories.
    I. Title II. Series
    823.9'14-dc23

ISBN-13: 978-0-7278-8303-2 (cased)

*All Severn House titles are printed on acid-free paper.*

Severn House Publishers support The Forest Stewardship Council [FSC],
the leading international forest certification organisation. All our titles that
are printed on Greenpeace-approved FSC-certified paper carry the FSC logo.

Typeset by Palimpsest Book Production Ltd.,
Falkirk, Stirlingshire, Scotland.
Printed and bound in Great Britain by
MPG Books Ltd., Bodmin, Cornwall.

# ONE

Gareth Cadwallader Owen, The Mamur Zapt, Head of the Khedive's Secret Police, was sitting in his office, the blinds drawn against the sun, grappling with the latest misdeeds of the Brotherhood, when Nikos, his official clerk, came in looking pale.

'Effendi . . .'

'Yes?'

'Miss Skiff to see you.'

Miss Skiff was the elderly and eccentric English lady who ran the Cairo Dispensary for Sick Animals.

Owen's responsibilities, although wide, did not in his view extend to sick animals. He turned back to the Brotherhood. 'You sort it,' he said.

After a while he became aware that Nikos was still standing there. 'Well?'

'She has a girl with her.'

'So?'

'A *little* girl,' said Nikos with emphasis.

Owen thought he understood. Nikos was not a family man. Owen sometimes suspected that his most intimate relationships were with the steel filing cabinets that filled his office. People, he was not good at; children, he could not make out at all. They filled him with alarm. He sometimes saw them from his window. They milled about in an unruly and unpredictable way. How did you deal with them? How, so to speak, did you come at them?

'Oh, very well,' said Owen, and got up from his desk. He went through into Nikos's office. Miss Skiff was sitting there with a little Egyptian girl, holding her by the hand.

'Captain Owen . . .'

Fraser, an engineer on the Egyptian railways, had been going along the carriages of the train that had just come in from

Luxor, checking the bearings for sand, when something had stirred in the darkness at the end of the carriage he was under. He crawled up to it and was surprised to find that it was a little girl squashed up in the space above the wheels. When he had hauled her out she had put up her hand to shield her eyes against the sudden brightness of the sun. And then the whole front of her face had fallen off.

'It gave me quite a turn,' he confessed afterwards at the bar.

Unnecessarily, it turned out, since what had come off was not in fact the front of her face but a dense layer of flies which had settled on a raw wound that they were concealing.

Still, that was bad enough and he felt that something ought to be done about it. But what?

'I mean, I had the rest of the train to examine,' he explained to his cronies at the bar.

'So what did you do?'

'Well, I thought at first of taking her to the hospital, but the Victoria is a long way from the Pont Limoun and, as I say, I had the rest of the train to do. But then I hit upon the answer. Miss Skiff's outfit is just up the road.'

'But that's for animals!'

'But she would know about wounds, wouldn't she? Anyway, I took the little girl along. I'll admit she was a bit surprised but she took her in. And I finished the train and went home for supper. Actually, I was a bit worried about it afterwards. I mean, you ought to report these things, oughtn't you? But to whom?'

'The police?'

'I suggested that to Miss Skiff, but she wasn't having any of it. Apparently, she had not got on too well with the police over some of her stray animals. And she had been talking to the girl, and said that was not the right thing to do. "This is a case for the Mamur Zapt," she said.'

The Mamur Zapt was a traditional post in the Egyptian government. Indeed, some claimed that he was the Khedive's right-hand man. Less traditionally, but like many of the other senior posts in the government, it was occupied today, in 1913, not by an Egyptian but by an Englishman. A few years before, the British had been invited to sort out Egypt's chaotic finances and, well, they had stayed. The effective ruler of Egypt was not the Khedive, nor his unfortunate Prime Minister, but the British High Commissioner who, in the interests of better administration – so he said – had installed his own British men in most of the country's senior posts. Including that of Mamur Zapt.

The present occupier of the post was not, actually, as he frequently but fruitlessly pointed out, an Englishman but a Welshman, which put him at a certain distance from both sides. He was loyal, or, as some claimed, disloyal to both sides. Anyway, in the High Commissioner's view – but not the Khedive's – this made for greater efficiency. In Owen's view it merely meant that he could be stabbed in the back by both sides.

'Hello!' said Owen. 'What's your name?'

The little girl was tongue-tied.

'Mine is Gareth,' he said easily. 'It's a funny name, I know, but that's because it's foreign. I come from England . . .' This was stretching a point, because he was Welsh and proud of it. 'Where do you come from?'

As she remained silent, he said, 'Let's see if I can guess: is it Luxor?'

The little girl shook her head.

'Assiut? No?'

He tried several other places.

'You've got me beat,' he said at last.

The little girl gave a triumphant smile. 'Denderah,' she whispered softly.

'Really? Well, that's a long way away! And you came all that way on the train? It can't have been very comfortable, under the train like that.' Nikos had showed him a briefing note as he came in. 'Was it dusty?'

The little girl nodded.

At least this man spoke in a language she could understand. Fraser had been totally incomprehensible to her.

'And the sand blew up, too, I expect. Did it get in your eyes?'

She nodded again.

'And in your mouth, I'll bet. Did you try to spit it out?'

He gave a mock spit. The little girl gazed at him, amazed. Then, tentatively, she followed suit.

Owen gave a yet bigger spit.

The little girl's face, so far as he could see it behind Miss Skiff's bandaging, broke into a delighted smile and she gave a huge spit.

They rivalled each other for a moment or two before Nikos's horrified eyes.

'Captain Owen . . .' Miss Skiff began.

'I'll bet you're thirsty after all that! Would you like a drink?'

On Nikos's desk, as in all offices in Cairo, was a pitcher of water. It was covered with a cloth, not just to keep out the sand, which came in through the shutters and lay in a thin film upon every surface, but to keep the water cool. A *suffragi* came in regularly and dipped the cloth in a bowl of ice and water and then wrapped it round the pitcher again.

Owen poured out a glass and gave it to the little girl.

'What did you say your name was?'

'Leila,' she said softly.

Gradually he teased her story out of her. Her mother had died giving birth to a little brother, who also had not lasted long. Her father had taken another wife and this time the wife was not so nice. For a time a bigger sister had protected her but then the sister had gone away. Then one day a white man had come and she had been told to go away with him.

'White man?' said Owen.

'Yes. But he wasn't very nice.' And there were other men, too, some with whips. And a lot of children like her. And they all started walking. And one of the men had said they were going to the sea and would get on a boat. But Leila had not wanted to go on a boat and had run away.

And now Owen understood why Miss Skiff had been so adamant that the little girl should be taken to the Mamur Zapt to tell her story.

*    *    *

'I thought the slave trade had been stamped out,' said Owen's friend Paul at the Sporting Club that evening. Paul was an ADC to the High Commissioner and Owen often found it useful to run things past him before they got out into the open and too many people had a hand in them.

'If it had been the Sudan, I would have understood it,' said Owen.

'Don't let them hear you saying things like that,' said Paul. 'They think they've stamped it out, too.'

The Sudan, that vast country, larger than India, which lay to the south of Egypt, was jointly governed by Egypt and Britain. There, too, there was a difference between appearance and reality. While formally the Sudan was a condominium, jointly governed by Egypt and Britain, in practice the British ran the show. Once their troops had re-conquered the Sudan – in the name of Egypt – some years before, the British had stayed there, too. It was Englishmen not Egyptians who were the District Commissioners and the country was governed from Khartoum. There, too, the slave trade had been put down – supposedly. It was one of the pretexts for the British invasion.

The Sudan had been the great slave market of Africa. Here traders had brought their captives from the south to be traded and sold on to the markets of the Middle East. Egypt had been one of those markets. In Egypt now the slave trade had been largely stamped out, though rumour had it that it still persisted in parts of the south, along the border with the Sudan.

The Sudan government hotly denied it and were zealous in their efforts to quash it, but the rumour persisted.

'I was thinking of having a word with their Slavery Bureau,' said Owen.

'It sounds as if you'd do better to have a word with *our* Slavery Bureau,' said Paul. 'If it still existed.'

The Egyptian Slavery Bureau had been abolished recently in the name of economy.

'My people won't want to hear about this,' said Paul. 'They think they've put slavery behind them, and won't want to restart the machinery for suppression. It's too costly.'

'So who do I have a word with?'

'A good question.'

'I thought you might—'

'Have a word with my boss? Yes. I will. But I'm not sure he'll want to know. Doing anything will cost money and he hasn't got any. Not until the next financial year.'

'It will be too late by then. They'd be out of Egypt.'

'It looks as if you're on your own, then.'

'Not me. It's really nothing to do with me. It's not political.'

The Mamur Zapt reckoned to concern himself only with political matters.

And meanwhile there was the question of what to do with Leila. Paul said that he thought they could find some institution which could look after her. Again, however, Miss Skiff was having none of it.

'They'd steal her back,' she said.

'*Steal* her?' The thought had not occurred to him.

'It would be better if she went home with you,' said Miss Skiff firmly.

Owen was not so sure about that. How would Zeinab react, for one thing?

He put it to her.

Zeinab was taken aback. She felt sorry for the child and wouldn't mind helping; but broad sympathy was one thing and having a child about the house where you would always be tripping over her was quite another. The prospect was faintly alarming.

Like Nikos, she was not used to children. She was the next best thing to an only child. She had a half-brother but he was much older than she was and they had never been close. Never, in fact, had much contact at all. He had not been around for years, hurried out of Egypt a while ago following an abortive attempt on the Khedive's life.

Zeinab was not, actually, Nuri Pasha's legitimate daughter. Her mother had been a famous courtesan who had resisted Nuri's repeated proposals of marriage, preferring to keep her independence. And her daughter had taken after her, insisting on cutting her own way through life. Nuri, modern-minded in some things, had gone along with this, seeing only that she received a proper (i.e. boy's) education along French lines. (Like many rich Egyptians he had no time for Egypt but plenty of time for France. England was a necessary evil.) Having done this he got out of the way and gave Zeinab her head. He had not frowned upon her relationship with Owen. There were, after all, advantages for a wily and eternally hopeful politician in having the Mamur Zapt as a sort of son-in-law.

But Zeinab had not exactly had a normal family upbringing. Nuri had doted on her as on her mother but had not actually had much to do with her. Her closest relationships had been with servants – or, in truth, with slaves – of whom, of course, given that this was a Pasha's household, there had been plenty. Not much difference, in fact, existed between slaves and servants. The result was that Zeinab, who thought of herself as a French liberal, was not too bothered about the slavery issue.

When she had moved in with Owen, she had not taken any slaves with her. Because of his special position, Owen, unusually among Europeans in Cairo, had no servants. Zeinab hadn't minded this. To her it was rather exotic, one of the many exotic things that had drawn her to Owen.

She had never had anything to do with children. Lately, one of her friends, Aisha, had had a baby. Zeinab had held it in her arms and, once she had got used to it, quite liked the experience. She wouldn't mind having a baby herself. In fact, at nearly thirty, perhaps she had better get on with it.

But having a grown child in the house was a bit different. She wasn't sure about that.

Not only that, the child was . . . different. She was, for a start, darker than Zeinab, or, indeed most Egyptians.

'She looks Sudani,' she said to Owen.

'She comes from Denderah,' he said. But he knew what Zeinab meant. Leila's features were not those of an Arab. But then, nor were those of many Egyptians. Still . . .

And then there was the question of colour. Again, this was not unusual among Egyptians, particularly those living in the south, where races had mixed over time. All the same, Leila's face was a bit . . . different.

Not that it mattered. The girl was only going to be with them for a short time. It was just that it was difficult for Zeinab to feel close to her. Not like a mother but, say, like an aunt. She told Leila to call her 'aunt'.

But there were practical things, too. What was the girl going to do all day? Zeinab hadn't the faintest idea. She consulted Aisha.

'Don't be daft!' said Aisha. 'Give her some things to play with. I'll let you have some of ours. And if you're really bothered, get someone in – a maid or a nurse or something.'

But that would mean having a servant in the house and Zeinab was not sure how Owen would feel about that.

Owen, as a matter of fact, was already toying with the idea. But for a different reason. He had been left uneasy by Miss Skiff's suggestion that the slavers might try to steal Leila back. What if they did that while he was out of the house?

He didn't want to have a guard. He had never gone in for guards and wasn't going to start now. But maybe, just while Leila was here . . .

An idea came to him. There was a man he knew, Musa, who had been in the police and whom Owen had borrowed on occasion and found reliable. He was now retired and working, so Owen had heard, as a part-time servant in several wealthy houses. People liked to employ ex-policemen in that capacity. There was some – well, better than none, anyway – guarantee of honesty and they were usually good at polishing things. Like ex-army people. Come to think of it, hadn't Musa served in the army as well? That might come in handy.

He sent for Musa and explained the situation to him. Musa would be glad to come, not just for the money but also for the prestige of working for the Mamur Zapt.

'Nights as well, Effendi? I can sleep on the floor.'

Owen thought. 'That might be a good idea,' he said.

Musa shuffled his feet. 'Can I bring my wife?' he asked. 'She would sleep on the floor, too,' he added quickly.

'I don't see why not. It would only be for a short time.'

There could even be other advantages to this. He knew that Zeinab felt uneasy at having a child around.

'Have you any children?' he asked.

'Three,' said Musa. 'But they're grown up now.'

'Would your wife mind looking after the girl?'

'She'd jump at the chance!' said Musa.

Zeinab's friend Aisha was married to a colleague of Owen's. Not exactly a colleague, since Mahmoud worked for the Parquet, and the Parquet, staffed by lawyers anxious to keep their distance from the government, and especially from the Mamur Zapt, whose legitimacy they (along with a lot of other people in Cairo, not all of them Egyptians) denied, tried to steer clear of anything to do with the Secret Police.

The Parquet was the Department of Prosecutions of the Ministry of Justice. The Egyptian system followed the French and not the British. Investigating a crime was the responsibility not of the police but of the Parquet. When a crime was committed, the police reported it to the Ministry of Justice, who passed it on to the Parquet to handle. The Parquet officer assigned to the case, a lawyer, looked into the matter and decided if there was a case to answer. If he thought there was he would bring the evidence together and present it to the Court. It was then his responsibility to prosecute and carry the case through to sentencing.

Mahmoud, one of the Parquet's bright young men, had just reached the stage in his career when things got difficult. That is, in Egypt, they got political. Egypt was a country of a multiplicity of nationalities, many religions, many diverse ethnic groups and several legal systems. There was the French-based national legal system, the Muslim law-based system, presided over by the Kadi, with its own independent laws and courts, and in addition a complicated financial and legal system known as the Capitulations, under which any citizen of another country could elect to be tried by a consular court set up by that country, answering to that country's law and judgements.

Enterprising criminals soon learnt the skills of switching rapidly from one nationality to another, delaying

the prosecution, the verdict and the consequences. The system
made the Parquet lawyers tear their hair out, and Egypt was
a great place for crooks.

What made the situation worse was for each consular court
there was, naturally, a consulate and a country. The effect
was to shift everything from the criminal to the political. You
could get so far and then the politicians, and their lawyers,
took over.

Mahmoud was just hitting these buffers. Owen, of course,
had hit them long before. Shared frustration had brought
Mahmoud and Owen together. At the most general level they
shared the same aim: justice – although Egyptians defined
that differently from the British. Mahmoud, a staunch Arab
Nationalist, didn't believe there should be such a thing as
the Mamur Zapt. Nor did the Khedive and nor, officially,
did the High Commissioner. It was just that, given the way
things were in Egypt, it was handy to have one around.

Despite all this, Mahmoud and Owen got on very well.

This morning Mahmoud had been assigned a new case, one
which reflected, he suspected, his declining value in the eyes
of his superiors. A goods train had come in from Luxor and
when the men went to unload it they had been put off by the
nasty smell emanating from one of the boxes.

'There's something dead in that,' Ali said to Hussein. 'You
mark my words!'

The box, which was about the size of a small trunk, was
sewn into a coarse canvas bag of the sort often used to
protect items in transit. You could almost have taken it, but
for its rectangular shape, for one of the larger Post Office
mail bags.

When they had lifted it out of the wagon and put it down
on the dusty sand, the smell was even more apparent, and
after it had been resting there for an hour or two – things did
not move fast in Egypt, particularly loading and unloading
– it became clear that the package was secreting fluid at one
end.

'Don't like the look of that,' Hussein said to Ali, giving the
box a wide berth and moving on to another one.

They continued giving it a wide berth and moving on to another one until there were no other ones for them to move on to.

'What about that one?' said the overseer, going past the box.

'Don't like the look of it,' said Ali.

'Don't like the smell of it,' said Hussein.

'What?' said the overseer, taken aback because Hussein and Ali had never shown signs of aesthetic or olfactory discrimination before.

He went up to the package and sniffed and looked and then he went to fetch the yard supervisor.

'There's something dead in there,' said the supervisor. 'Who's the package for?'

He instructed the overseer to read the label. The overseer would have instructed someone else to read the label, since the smell now was quite overpowering. However, neither Ali nor Hussein could read and he knew that the clerk would refuse to move out of his office, so, with the greatest reluctance, he approached the box himself.

'Can't read it,' he announced. 'It's for a Pasha somebody or other.'

'Look, just find out who it is and then we'll get them to send someone to come and move it.'

The overseer reluctantly approached the package again. 'It's like I said: you can't read it. It's been soiled by . . . Well, it's been soiled, anyway.'

'Of course you can read it! Someone must be able to read it!'

Others were pressed into trying but without success.

'Look, we can't just leave the box there, not the way it is. I mean, people have to go past,' said the supervisor.

'And some of us have to go past a lot,' said Ali and Hussein.

'It's what's inside it,' said the overseer.

'We can't just leave it there,' the supervisor said again. 'We'll have to move it.'

But where to? Anywhere else in the yard would just move the problem rather than solve it; and if the package was just moved out of the yard and dumped, as they were tempted to do, this would almost certainly cause trouble too. And plenty of it, if the box did indeed belong to a Pasha.

'We're going to have to open it,' said the supervisor with decision. 'It's probably a dead dog or something.'

'Yes,' said Ali, more cheerfully now there was a prospect of something happening. 'Probably sent up from his estate or something.'

'A prize dog!' said Hussein enthusiastically. 'A hunting dog. A Saluki maybe. He wanted it sent up to him!'

'And the bastards put it in a box with no air and no water! Just sealed it up and sent it off!'

'A prize dog, too! Now if it had been an ordinary dog—'

'And not a Pasha's dog. There'll be trouble over this, you mark my words! He'll kick their backsides for this!'

'Well, they deserve kicking! Ignorant bastards! But that's what they're like down there in the south.'

'Sudanis, I shouldn't wonder,' said Hussein.

'Are you going to open that box or not?' demanded the overseer.

Not, was the answer they would have preferred. But jobs were jobs and someone had to do it, and if it was a nasty job or a dirty job, it was usually them.

So . . . When the cloth covering was cut away and removed it revealed a cheap, gaudily decorated box, painted in all the colours of the rainbow.

'Why!' said Ali. 'It's a—'

'Bride box,' finished Hussein.

And when Mahmoud opened the box later, he saw that the bride was inside.

Bride boxes were perhaps less common than they had once been but no respectable girl, especially in Upper Egypt, would consider getting married without one. In it she accumulated her trousseau and when the great moment came would transfer with it to the bridegroom's house. She would build it up over the years and as the wedding approached it would become more and more prominent. In the days immediately before the wedding the world would be invited round to gaze and wonder.

You could buy one in the souk, of course, or have one made especially for you. The painting was done by a separate skilled, or possibly not so skilled craftsman. The craftsman was probably also responsible for the gaudy paintings, usually of trees and reeds, which appeared on the front of houses and showed that the owner had performed a pilgrimage to Mecca.

The present box was empty except for the person lying there, a young woman. So much could be made out but little more. The corpse had been so distended by the heat and the gases that it was practically unrecognizable. It could not have been in the bride box for more than three days. Otherwise its presence would have become even more unpleasantly obvious. Nor, probably, would it have been there for less than two days. He would check the documentation and see when the box had been picked up.

Almost certainly it would have come from the south. Mahmoud sighed. That would mean he would have to go down there to make inquiries. Like most Cairenes, especially the educated ones, the proposal of travelling down to the south filled him with horror. It was so hot there, especially at this time of the year. And so uncomfortable, so lacking in normal creature comforts. Like showers, or so he had heard. Mahmoud, though highly intelligent and educated, was not above the prejudices common to the Cairo intelligentsia: that civilizatio began and ended in Cairo, with a possible branch line Alexandria. Anywhere else, though, and especially anywhe in the south, was not just beyond the pale of civilization, was positively primeval.

Perhaps he could start his inquiries at the other end: v the label and with the man, if only he could make it ou whom it was addressed.

He had the body sent round to the morgue for a post-mo The box would just have to stay where it was for the being. If it was taken to the Parquet offices, especially present state, he would be highly unpopular. He wasn't to send it round to a police station because it would dis and most likely reappear in the souk, where it would be up and then used again. People were cheap in Cair

was cheaper to leave the bride box where it was and post a guard than try to find space for it somewhere else. But he would take the label and show it to the experts.

Musa had moved into Owen's house with Latifa, his wife. She had arrived carrying a bed roll containing all the possessions they would need. They installed themselves in the kitchen, which wasn't used much. Both Owen and Zeinab were usually out for lunch and in the evening they went round the corner to a restaurant they favoured. Owen could usually rustle up a very basic meal if it was required. Zeinab would usually send for one of her father's cooks. Owen, however, thought that this was excessive and they usually reserved that for a special occasion, when for instance, they had guests. Zeinab had a Pasha's daughter's tastes but on an English official's income. Reason, said Owen, ought to prevail in these things. So it did, said Zeinab; only her reason not his.

Latifa at once took over responsibility for Leila. This was a great relief to Zeinab, who couldn't think what she was going to do with her otherwise. It was Latifa who had discovered that Leila really was a Sudani. That explains it, thought Zeinab, who shared the universal Cairene view that all bad things came from the south.

Not that there was much bad about Leila. For the first day or two she crouched in a corner of the kitchen sucking her thumb. After a few attempts to draw her out, Latifa stopped trying. Instead, she just got on with some cooking. That wasn't strictly part of the contract but she did it anyway. She said she couldn't just sit there idle, and anyway, her man needed his meals. Needed them, too, in a way that only she could perform. So she got to work at the centre table, and, over in the corner, Leila sat watching her, and gradually she was drawn in.

'What sort of family is she from?' Latifa said to Owen. 'She don't know nothing!'

So Latifa set about teaching her.

'Her mother dead,' she said to Owen the next day. 'No time to teach. Sister not know much more than she. What sort of family? And now the new wife sit on her ass all day and try

look pretty! But what her father doing? Musa like that and he out of the door! But with new wife, that all he think about. But what about children? Hah! Want get rid of them. They mean nothing to him. Hah!' she finished, with disgust.

Fortunately, Musa wasn't like that. He took his time with Leila, not forcing things, after the first attempts, but content, like Latifa, to wait. And gradually Leila got used to him and occasionally ventured a word when together they were cutting up the onions for Latifa. She even helped Musa to polish the brass and copperware that had never been polished before. Musa let her help him, although, really, he believed that this was a job for a man. It needed the strength and stamina of the ex-soldier – the way he did it.

'Like buttons, like belt,' he said. 'Polished till you can see your face.'

Owen was glad to have him in the house. He didn't think that the traders would really go to the trouble of snatching Leila back but all the same, the possibility worried him. He would be glad to hand the problem over to . . .

And that was the problem: to whom? Paul had come back to him asking him to stay with it until his boss had made up his mind. He was thinking about it. There were aspects beyond the ken of ordinary mortals. Chief amongst these was that His Majesty's Government was anxious, as always, to cut costs – and among the costs they were thinking of cutting was that of the Slave Bureau in the Sudan. The slave trade was dead and buried, surely? The Bureau was no longer needed, surely? And still less any possible corresponding unit in Egypt, where the slave trade was even deader.

Or so it had seemed. Until this.

What his boss really wanted, said Paul, was for someone to quickly wrap the whole thing up. Then they could go away and forget about it. Just get on with what they had been doing. Carrying through the cuts.

'He thinks you might be the man to do it,' said Paul, 'especially as it has, in a way, landed in your lap.'

'That was just fortuitous,' said Owen.

'Things that land in your lap fortuitously,' said Paul, 'have a way of staying there.'

'I have a lot of other things in my lap at the moment,' said Owen. 'Things with the potential to turn into hot potatoes. Political things. Which is my job.'

'And you think that this is not political?' said Paul neutrally, gazing away into the distance.

Owen went to the Central Station at Pont Limoun, taking Leila with him. He wanted to go over it again with her. He also wanted to talk to some of the people. In particular, he wanted to talk with Fraser.

On their way they passed the goods platform. The bride box was still standing there.

Leila pulled at his hand. 'Why,' she said, 'that's Soraya's box!'

# TWO

'And Soraya is . . .?' prompted Mahmoud.

As soon as Owen had established from the guard who it was that had posted him beside the box, Owen had sent for him and Mahmoud had come running.

'My sister,' whispered Leila. 'My big sister,' she had added after a moment, proudly.

Mahmoud looked at Owen. Owen knew what he was thinking. The obvious thing to do was to get Leila to identify the girl who lay in the box, but he shrank from that.

'Tell us about your sister,' said Owen.

On that subject the hesitant Leila was forthcoming. Her sister was bigger than her, a lot bigger. She had looked after her when their mother had died, had stood up for her against the new mother. And against their father. To such an extent that her father had hit her. Their new mother had hit her too and said that she couldn't have her in the house and that she would have to go. And, soon after, she went.

'Where to?' asked Mahmoud.

Leila didn't know. But the next day her box was taken away so Leila presumed she had gone to get married.

Had Leila gone to the wedding feast?

No, she hadn't, and she had been rather disappointed at that. Usually when someone got married there was singing and dancing and feasting; the whole village was involved. But there had been nothing like that this time. When Leila had got up in the morning, Soraya had disappeared – without even saying goodbye to her, which Leila found odd and which had made her feel sad.

Had her parents said anything?

No, just that she had gone and that she wouldn't be coming back. When Leila had asked where she had gone to, her new mother had said, 'A long way away.' Leila had been sorry about that because she had hoped she would go on seeing her sister. Indeed, she confided, she had half hoped that Soraya would take her with her and that she could stay with her permanently. She had even suggested this to her father but he had just laughed. And, soon after, she had been sent away herself.

'Tell us about that,' said Owen.

A man had come and gone off with her father and they had been drinking. She always knew when her father had been drinking because when he came back he was red in the face and shouted a lot. This time, he had come into the house and shouted for her new mother and when she had come out they had sent Leila off and her father had fetched more beer. When Leila had returned some time later they had been still drinking, her new mother, too, and Leila had gone to bed. Well, not to bed, because they didn't have one. In the house it was too noisy and they had shouted at her to keep away. So she had curled up in a corner of the yard and slept there. And in the morning her father had woken her and said that she was to get ready. 'There's no need for her to get ready,' her new mother had said. 'She doesn't have a box; she can go as she is.' And, later in the morning, a man had come for her.

'Was this the white man?' asked Owen.

'White man?' said Mahmoud.

No, just an ordinary fellah, like the fellah in the village, only he didn't come from the village, or not their village at any rate. The man had come and taken her to a place outside the village where the white man was waiting. He had looked her over carefully and then nodded, and then she had been led to where a group of children were waiting with other men.

'A group of children?' said Mahmoud.

'Yes.'

How many?

Leila had a problem with that. She thought about fifteen.

'And then?'

'They had all started walking.'

'This is a bad family,' whispered Mahmoud. 'They drink, and they do not fear God.'

Mahmoud, a good Muslim, never drank.

'And they beat their children. And – I think you are right – they sell them as slaves. What sort of people are these?'

'Worse,' said Owen. 'What did they do to the sister?'

'You think they killed her?'

'I think they might have done. Were they going to sell her, too? And did she stand up against it? It sounds, from what Leila says, like she was the sort of girl who might. There could have been blows.'

Mahmoud nodded. 'That does not sound unlikely,' he said and sighed. 'It sounds as if I'm going to have to go down south,' he said.

'Me too,' said Owen.

They solved the problem of identification by getting Leila to describe the clothing her sister normally wore. There wasn't a lot of it, even when you took into account what had been in the bride box. And then Mahmoud had taken a less soiled piece of the clothing the woman in the box had been wearing and showed it to Leila.

'Like this?'

Leila had nodded. She didn't really understand the purport of the questions but they were making her uneasy. Mahmoud had thought it best not to go on.

'The body will keep,' he said to Owen, 'now that it's in the mortuary. I'll get somebody from down there to identify it.'

But where was 'there'? The little girl had said Denderah. That was certainly a place, and they would try it. It was also on the main line to Luxor. It was where she could have got on the train. And possibly where the bride box had been put on, too. If it was, there would be a record of some sort of it. The Egyptian bureaucracy was not always efficient but it was always there. Even in such a one-horse town as Owen suspected Denderah was.

It would especially have been recorded if it was addressed to a Pasha, if for no other reason than that if you got it wrong, thunderbolts would fall.

But this was another thing that they both found puzzling:

that the body should be boxed up and sent, as it apparently
had been done, to a Pasha. Wasn't that the last thing you would
do if you murdered somebody? Suppose, for instance, that
Owen's theory was correct and that Soraya had been killed
by a bunch of slave traders: would they want to draw attention
to themselves? It was, surely, the last thing that they would
want to do.

But didn't the same argument apply if what Mahmoud
had originally feared was correct? That this was a dull,
ordinary murder, domestic, probably, in an ordinary town
very much out in the sticks, just the sort of case that you
would be assigned to if your career was on the point of
plunging irrevocably downwards? Suppose it was – surely
the very last thing a murderer would do would be to draw
attention to it?

Unless there was some ulterior motive. Mahmoud feared
there might be. And he half feared that the motive was to do
with him personally. Mahmoud was on the progressive side
of Egyptian politics, which was a lonely place to be. It brought
him right up against the most vested interests that there were
in Egyptian society, those that were based around the Court
and around the Pashas. The one thing they did not want was
to have those interests questioned or exposed. But so often
Mahmoud had found that they were precisely the thing that
made progress impossible.

Mahmoud believed deeply, passionately, in progress. It
galled him that Egypt was seen as backward, primitive, locked
in the past. It had to modernise – *had* to! He had fought for
that throughout his career and was just beginning to believe
that he was on the point of getting somewhere.

And there, of course, lay the snag. For his efforts were
beginning to bring him against the most powerful interests of
all. They were beginning to notice him; and, no doubt, starting
to do something about it.

This case could be the beginning. An obscure case, miles
from anywhere. And then the block on it. The introduction of
a Pasha into it was the clue. It would stop the inquiry, as it
always did. Not completely. Just enough to keep him tied up
forever in some backwater down there.

For Owen, too, the entrance of a Pasha into the case was something to make him think. If this really was something to do with the slave trade – an indication, perhaps, of its revival in Egypt – did the connection with a Pasha mean that there were big forces behind it? It was profitable enough to tempt even Pashas. And what about Leila's mention of white men: how far did this go?

'Political enough for you yet?' he could hear Paul saying.

'I told you it was big,' Ali said to Hussein. 'The Mamur Zapt *and* the Parquet!'

'Must be a prize dog!' said Hussein.

'A Saluki at least!'

'Shouldn't have put it in a box like that!' said Hussein.

'Without any air!'

'The Pasha will have the skin off them!'

'And they'll deserve it!'

'Ought to know better!'

'Ignorant sods down there!'

'Are you two ever going to do any work?' asked the overseer.

'Coming, coming!'

Hussein and Ali bent to the box. They straightened up again.

'Heavy!'

'Too heavy!'

'Look, they've taken the dog out of it. So I gather. It'll be lighter than it was!' said the overseer.

'It's more than a two-man lift.'

'Four men at least!'

'Look, it's only down to the Bab-el-Khalk!'

'In this heat?'

'Just get on with it! Or it won't be the Pasha who flays your hide!'

'Bastard!' muttered Ali.

'Bastard!' muttered Hussein.

'Right! Lift!'

They raised it an inch.

'Can't be done!'

'Not with just two of us.'

'A bride box? Of course it can be done!'

'Not just with two of us.'

'All right. I'll get Abdul.'

'And Mustapha.'

'Mustapha's doing something else.'

'We'll wait.'

'I'm going to fetch Abdul *and* Mustapha. And then I'm going to kick your backsides.'

The overseer went off in a fury.

Ali and Hussein sat down on the ground in the shade of the box.

'Doesn't smell as bad as it did.'

'You fancy? It's still pretty bad.'

'Maybe it's just that I'm getting used to it.'

'You do get used to things, don't you? This box, for instance, I've got used to seeing it here. I shall quite miss it when it goes.'

'Well, I shan't!' said the guard Mahmoud had posted. 'It's really hot just standing here. *And* I can still smell it. *And* it smells pretty bad!'

'Stop complaining! You don't have to carry it.'

'You just have to stand there.'

'All day,' said the guard. 'All day. *And* all night!'

'I'll bet you don't stand there all night!'

'Well, no one would expect me to. But I'm still on guard.'

'With his eyes closed!'

'I would know if anyone tried to make off with it.'

'You'd probably have tipped them off. Then down in the souk with it and split the money!'

'A bride box?'

'Well, there's always a demand for them. Girls are always getting married.'

'Yes, well, most girls don't put dogs in them!'

'Hello, here are Abdul and Mustapha!'

'This it? We're not expected to carry this down to the Bab-el-Khalk, are we?'

'Yes, you bloody are!' said the overseer. 'Four of you! Why, I could carry it there myself!'

'Go on, show us!'

'I'll show you something else in a minute! Now bloody get on with it!'

They bent and lifted.

'Hey! What are you doing with my sister's box?' said Leila indignantly. She had just come up the platform with Owen and Mahmoud.

The men put the box down.

'Your sister's, is it?' one of the guards said. 'Well, it needs a bit of a clean.'

'It was all right when she took it away!'

'Well, that was then, and this is now. It's had something in it since. Something which doesn't smell too good.'

'What the hell do you think it can be?' said Abdul, sniffing.

'I reckon a rat's got in there,' said Mustapha.

'Got in and stayed, by the smell of it!'

'A pretty big-sized rat, it must be.'

'We reckon it was a dog. It's addressed to a Pasha, see. And we reckon it's one of his prize dogs. Must be, for them to go to the trouble.'

'A dog!' said Leila, bursting into tears. 'In my sister's box?'

The men looked at each other uncomfortably.

'It's not right, you know,' said Abdul. 'You shouldn't do that to a girl's bride box.'

'It's special,' said Mustapha. 'It means a lot to her.'

'Do you know what I think?' said Abdul. 'I reckon the Pasha came along and said: "I need a box. That one will do." So they just tipped everything out and put the dog inside.'

'They shouldn't do that!' said Leila, crying. 'It's my sister's bride box!'

'No more they should!' said Abdul. 'These Pashas are bastards!'

'Think they can get away with anything!' said Mustapha.

'Bastards!' all four men agreed.

'But what about my sister's things? They were beautiful things. She'd made them herself!'

'Yes, well, that's how it is,' said Abdul, with a sympathy surprising since this was only a girl.

'Don't worry!' said Mustapha. 'The people in the village will have picked them up.'

'And gone off with them, I shouldn't be surprised,' said Hussein.

'If they have, her husband will get them back,' said Abdul. '"Give them back or I'll beat your head in," he'll say. And you'll be surprised at the effect it will have.'

'They ought not to have done it,' said Leila. 'It's my sister's box!'

When it was hot, really hot, for it was always hot in Cairo, they slept on the roof. They had fenced off a garden area with trellis work up which they had trained beans. Beans were grown for decoration as well as food in Egypt. On the roof they served as a dense, green screen, with occasional splashes of red from the flowers. Behind the screen they were invisible to the sleepers on neighbouring roofs, like them in search of air during the hot nights.

The drawback was that you woke with the sun. Zeinab merely pulled the sheet over her head and carried on sleeping. But Owen was fully awake from the moment the first sun touched his face. He always was.

This morning he got up and walked to the edge of the roof and looked out over the still, sleeping city to where the Nile curved round the houses and the hawks were already beginning to hover on the upward currents of air. Below him, in the little nearby gardens, the doves were beginning to gurgle in the trees. He always loved this moment of the day before the city woke up, when all was still and quiet and the air fresh, sometimes with dew.

Sometimes, as now, it was even chilly. At least, you could imagine that, and people, English men especially, nostalgic for home, often liked to do that. In the evening you sometimes even lit a fire, which you never really needed to do, but it was nice to imagine it on a frosty morning in England and to stretch out your hands and feel the warmth. Of course, there was warmth all the time but this was a different warmth. He didn't need that today, though. Already the heat was beginning to build up. Already, over the Nile, there were little heat shimmers.

All the same, he pulled on his cotton dressing gown. In the

pocket he felt something. He pulled it out. It was a little *trocchee* shell and it had been found clutched in the girl's fingers when they had conducted the post-mortem.

He had shown it to Mahmoud and Mahmoud had asked him where it came from.

'Probably Flamenco Bay,' he had said. 'That's where most of them come from.'

Flamenco Bay was a little to the north of Port Sudan and was where the red, green, and yellow-painted dhows unloaded their cargoes of trocchee shells in hundreds of thousands.

'The shells go to the United States and to France, where they're cut up into buttons. Most of the pearl buttons that you see come from Flamenco Bay.'

He had told Mahmoud to smell it.

'That's awful!' said Mahmoud. 'It smells like rotten fish!'

'It *is* rotten fish. They sort of stew inside the shells. The sun rots them, and then they drop out. But the smell! You should smell it in Flamenco Bay!'

'I'd rather not!'

'They grind them up into a powder. There's a steady demand for it in Arabia.

'As a fertilizer?'

Owen smiled.

'As an aphrodisiac.'

It was a button, here, one they had found in Soraya's hand.

Pulled off from her assailant? That didn't necessarily mean that the attacker had been a woman. Men wore pearl buttons as well, sometimes on their shirts, if they were posh, on their *galabeyas* if they were not. Even sometimes among the beads on their skull caps.

Soraya had fought before they killed her. They had had to stun her with a blow. And then they had strangled her. The body had decomposed badly in the heat of the box, but the pathologist had been able to make this out.

Owen was wondering how to tell Leila. He would tell her very little, as little as he could.

He would have to show her the button and ask her if she recognized it. It could have come from Soraya's own clothes.

But somehow he didn't think it did. It had been ripped off.
Did you do that to your own clothes? It was more likely that
Soraya, who seemed to have been a girl of spirit, had fought
back.

The question, though, was whether the button told you more.
Trocchee buttons were everywhere in Egypt. But they were
most plentiful, naturally enough, along the Red Sea coast,
where they came from. There everyone wore them.

Did that indicate that her attacker had come from round
there? The Sudan? Not Egypt.

More; could that mean that that was where she was being
taken? As a slave, along with her little sister, and other
children. First, to a port on the Red Sea – Port Sudan, say
– where the control was not as tight as it was in Egypt, and
where boats, Arab boats, came and went every day in large
numbers? Once there it would be easy to put children on an
incoming dhow just after it had dropped its cargo, of trocchee
shells, possibly, and then sail them over to the other side of
the Red Sea and on to the still existing slave markets of the
Middle East. Was that where Leila – and possibly Soraya
– had been bound?

That morning the first thing he did when he got into his office
at the Bab-el-Khalk was to get Nikos to issue a general instruction to the police station and customs offices of south Egypt
alerting them to the possible passage of a slave caravan with
children. The Mamur Zapt had few officers of his own; but
you ignored his direct instructions at your peril.

Of course, the slavers would be keeping to the desert and
giving towns and police as wide a berth as possible. They
might even have an arrangement with some police forces.
That he could do nothing about. In fact, trying to pick the
caravan up in the desert was worse than looking for a needle
in a haystack. The distances were vast and there was no
question of combing the desert. He just didn't have enough
men to do that. The time to intercept them was when they
were coming to the coast and looking for their port. The
trouble was that that might be anywhere along the Red Sea
coast.

He sat thinking for a moment and then gave the Navy a call. They didn't have many ships and the sea was even more vast than the desert. But Navy ships patrolled the area regularly looking for gunrunners and they could just as well look for children as for guns.

And then he put in a call to the Sudan Slavery Bureau in Khartoum.

Mahmoud's experts thought they had at last deciphered the address on the box's label.

'An illiterate scrawl,' they sniffed. 'And badly soiled.'

However, they thought the box had been directed to the Pasha Ali Maher, so Mahmoud went to see him.

'A bride box?' said Ali Maher incredulously. 'Not much call for them up here!'

'You don't, perhaps, collect such objects? As antiques, possibly?'

'No, I don't!' said the Pasha, waving a hand at the exquisite furnishing and objects that surrounded them. Even Mahmoud could see that the carpets that hung on the walls (you put carpets on the walls, not on the floors in Egypt, where the floors were cooler marble) were soft and luxurious and, in his terms, pretty well priceless.

'A bride box.' Ali Maher smiled and looked around at the lovely blue vases, probably Chinese, and the jade pieces standing discreetly in niches around the room. 'No, I don't think so. I don't go in for primitive art.'

They were talking in French. Cairo's upper classes felt more at home in that language than in Arabic. Come to that, they felt more at home on the airy Riviera than in sweaty Cairo and spent as much time as they could in France.

Mahmoud had no problem with French. The Egyptian legal system was based on the Code Napoleon – an earlier Khedive who admired all things French, especially the women, had taken French law as the model when he had reformed the system. The lectures in the School of Law were all in French. Meetings in the Parquet were usually conducted in French; memoranda were usually written in French, occasionally in English but hardly ever in Arabic. Arabic was a tricky language to write and on the whole the Parquet preferred to keep the records in French. At home Mahmoud spoke Arabic; with his colleagues he usually spoke French (and either French or English when he was speaking to Owen; they both were at ease in both).

So Mahmoud was not bothered by Ali Maher's assumption that they would converse in French. It was the language of all the Egyptian upper classes. You could almost say that he was treating Mahmoud as an equal.

But Mahmoud knew he wasn't. There was a subtle condescension about everything Ali Maher said or did. It was as if merely receiving Mahmoud in his house was doing him a favour. Parquet officers did not rate high with Pashas.

'It seems odd that the box should be specifically addressed to you,' said Mahmoud.

'A simple mistake, I expect,' said Ali Maher languidly. 'They happen all the time in this benighted country. Where did you say it came from? The south? Oh, well, that explains it! The people there are backward. Blockheads, most of them. Some oaf has just got it wrong.' He shook his head. 'A bride box? To me?' He laughed. 'Now, if it had been a bride or two, I could understand!'

It was then that Mahmoud told him what the box had contained.

He was watching Ali Maher closely and would have sworn that the Pasha lost colour. He pulled out a silk handkerchief and wiped his brow.

'How ghastly!' he said.

'Does this put a different complexion on it?'

Ali Maher looked puzzled. 'No, I don't think so,' he said. 'No, I don't think so. Why should it?'

'Addressed to you. Meant for you. You personally.'

'I'm afraid I don't see . . .'

'Not a mistake,' said Mahmoud.

'Not a mistake?'

'A threat, perhaps. Or a warning.'

'Why should it be any of those things?'

'I don't know. I was hoping that perhaps you would tell me.'

'I can see no reason why it should be either of those things.'

'There is no one who might wish to harm you? Who has reason to feel hostile towards you?'

'Well, of course, as a public figure . . .'

'Down in the south?'

'Well, that's a big area . . .'

'Near Denderah, say?'

'Denderah? Well, I have heard of it. But, no, I don't think so. I try to have as little to do with such places as I can.'

'You have no connections with the place?'

'No. I would try to avoid having any connections with anywhere like that.'

'Or persons . . .?'

Ali Maher held up his hand. 'Young man,' he said, 'why go on? Is it not obvious that this is a simple mistake? What could I possibly have to do with a woman in a box?'

But was it Denderah? Leila had certainly said so. That was where she lived, she had said, and if she had lived there presumably her sister had done too. That was where the box had started. Or had it? Leila had thought that was the name of her village but she was a little girl and had not been too sure. Owen tried to question her about the village, but it seemed a village like any other: houses, a street (sort of), a kind of square. Doum palms. A water wheel pulled by an ox. The river? Not far away but the village had not been quite on the river.

That was where she had lived and thought she had got on the train. When she had slipped away, in the late night or early morning, from the other children, evading the guard, she had walked and walked. She didn't know the way; she had just followed the tracks the caravan had made. It was easy. There were no other tracks to confuse her. The caravan had kept away from other people.

So she had walked and walked, and been very hungry and thirsty, but a woman had given her a bowl of durra and let her have a drink from her water skin. And she had gone on walking until she had seen her village. She had intended to go back to her house but she had met a woman, a neighbour, who had recognized her, and said that she should not go back because her mother would beat her again.

She hadn't known what to do. She had asked the woman, Khabradji, if she knew where Soraya was, and the woman had clicked her tongue and said no. She could well be a long way away by this time. Khabradji had given her some water and some bread and had let her sleep in the sand behind her house but had said she must be gone by morning or her man would be angry.

So Leila had gone to sleep behind the house, but she had been cold in the middle of the night and had woken up. As she was lying there she had heard the train and the thought had come to her that she might get on it and go far away, far away from her nasty new mother and from the white man and the men with whips.

And she had walked over to where she knew the train would be. It was dark and no one had seen her. The train had stopped and the driver had got out and was squatting at a brazier with the other men. And they were drinking tea.

And another man was doing something to the engine. He had climbed up on to the top of it and had swung across – she wasn't quite sure what he had swung across; it was like a huge arm – and he had put one end of it into the engine and then said 'Taib!' – arabic for 'it is well' – and another man, who was standing beside a sort of tall tower, to which the arm was attached, had also said 'Taib', and then there had been a gurgle as of water, and she thought the train might have been drinking. Well, that would be reasonable, wouldn't it? A train needed a drink, like everyone else. And after a while it had stopped drinking and the man had swung the arm back, the driver had got back into his cab, and Leila had guessed that the train was soon going to start, so she had crept under a carriage and found a place.

Owen asked her about the station. What station? There wasn't one, not a big one as in Cairo. There was no platform or anything. There was just a little building for 'the man' and the water tower. And the piles of gum arabic stacked beside the line to be picked up by a goods train at some point.

When people came – yes, people did come; she had seen them on other occasions – they took a horse and carriage and drove into the town. The drivers knew they were coming and shortly before the train arrived the carriages would draw up. Sometimes the people rode on donkeys.

There were often a lot of people. The ladies were 'Inglesi', although not all of them were English, and they wore beautiful long dresses and big hats and looked beautiful. Although they were sometimes very hot. Even under the hats the sweat was running down their faces. And they were forever calling for water. And the men wore suits and they also had big hats, although different ones.

And what did they go into the village to see?

Leila shuddered. 'The Place of the Giants,' she said.

From what she said it sounded like a temple. Was there a temple at Denderah? He rather thought there was. He would have to ask McPhee, the Assistant Commissioner, who was interested in such things.

But there were many places with temples in Egypt.

He asked her about this one.

Yes, she had been there. But she didn't like it. It was frightening. Big and dark, although it had got lighter since the Pasha had ordered some of the sand to be cleared away. But it was still dark and there were lots of places from which boys could jump out at you. But even they were frightened, she thought. The fact was, it was not a good place. It was not a decent, holy place, not a good Muslim place. There were spirits there, bad spirits. And you knew that was so because – she crept closer to Owen and whispered in his ear – of the magic marks. Right up there on the front, for everyone to see!

Owen went in to see McPhee to check if there was a temple at Denderah. This was a mistake since once the Assistant Commissioner got started on Egyptian antiquities you couldn't get him to stop.

'Ah, Denderah!' he said reminiscently. 'The Temple of Hathor. It's very late, you know. Roman. The earliest name you find there is Cleopatra, that vile woman!'

'Oh, really? You feel that, do you?'

'Definitely! Sexually abandoned.'

'Well, I've always thought that—'

'No, no, Owen. You have a romantic view of her. That's Shakespeare's doing. "The chair she sat in . . ." You know, that sort of stuff. A marvellous picture, but quite untrue. She sold herself for power, you know!'

'Well, if you're going to sell yourself, that might be worth doing it for.'

'No, no, Owen. It's her *honour* she's selling as well as her body.'

McPhee had always seemed to Owen to have a Boy Scout's view of life.

He put Cleopatra reluctantly to one side.

'Apparently the temple has some unusual markings . . .'

'Oh, yes, the famous Zodiac.'

'Famous Zodiac?'

'Yes, on the portico. You see, the sign of the Lion comes first, showing that the summer solstice was then in that sign. Not like now, of course, when it's in Cancer.'

'Oh, really?'

'At Esne the sign of Virgo comes first.'

'Extraordinary! Well, I'd better be getting along . . .'

'Of course, this shows that in Egypt the precession of the equinoxes was already well known.'

'It does?'

'Of course, it may simply be that the Egyptian astronomers wanted to represent two successive states of the sky—'

'Yes, yes. Well, thank you. I'm afraid that now I must be—'

'That in which the summer solstice was in Leo, and consequently the Vernal equinox in Taurus, instead of Aries.'

'Yes, yes, most interesting. But I'm afraid I—'

'As opposed to that in which the summer solstice was in Virgo and consequently the vernal equinox in Gemini.'

'*Most* interesting. Well, I must be getting along . . .'

'Champollion thinks—'

'Yes, yes, thank you. Thank you. I'm afraid I have to be . . .'

He edged out of the door.

They could be Leila's 'magic marks'! In which case, yes, the halt where she had got on the train was at Denderah. And Denderah was the village she came from.

# THREE

'A bride box?' said the clerk at Denderah station doubtfully. 'No, Effendi, I do not remember a bride box. And, surely, if there had been one, I would have remembered it. They are not things you see every day. And usually, Effendi, a bride goes with it. A woman does not like to be parted from her box. Surely if there had been a box, there would have been a bride. There would have been singing and dancing and much merriment. A thing like that I could not but have marked. But there has been nothing like that here!'

'I think it is possible,' said Mahmoud, 'that the two were separated in this case, the bride and her box. And you might not have recognized it as a bride box, for it was stitched into a bag. Like this one here.'

He pointed to a package in the mail bag behind the clerk's desk. 'Only much bigger, of course. This big!' He spread his arms.

'In that case it would not have been with the ordinary mail, then. All parcels have to be weighed, and that would be too big to be weighed on these scales. It would have to be weighed on the weighing machine I use for commercial packages: oil cakes and such things. And now I think I remember . . . Come with me, Effendis. It should be on the list.'

He led them to a little goods shed, in which was a large weighing machine. Beside it was a list pinned to a board.

'Yes, I thought so. It was your mention of a bride box that led me astray. For this was no bride box, Effendi. A bride box must be treated with respect and the men who brought this had no respect. "This is to go on the train," they said. "How can it?" I said. "When it does not even have a label!" "Label?" they said. "What is that?" They were ignorant men, Effendis. Fellahin from the field.

"'A label," I said, "is to show where the parcel is to go to. It is a piece of paper," I said, seeing that they still did not understand. "Like this."

"'It has writing on it!" they said.

"'Well, yes," I said. "It would have." They conferred among themselves. "Do it, then!" they said. For, Effendis, there was not one among them who could read and write.

"'Very well, then," I said. "But you will have to tell me what to put. First, who is it to go to?"

"'The Pasha," they said.

"'Which Pasha?" I asked.

"'Our Pasha."

"'Look," I said, "there are Pashas all over the place. What is his name?"

"'Our Pasha," they said. "Ali Maher."

"'Right," I said. "And where is this to go to?"

"'His house."

"'His house where? He has dozens."

"'His big house. In the city."

"'Cairo, yes?"

"'Yes, Cairo."

"'The street?" I asked.

"'Street?" they repeated.

"'The name of the road in which he lives," I explained. They looked at each other.

"'Surely if it says it is the Pasha Ali Maher, that will do?" they said. I sighed.

"'There are hundreds of Pashas in Cairo," I explained. "And hundreds of streets."

"'Hundreds of streets?"

"'Look," I said. "I'll put down *The Pasha, Ali Maher*. And maybe it will get to him. Right, now what is it?" I asked. They spoke among themselves.

"'What is that to you?" they said. And looked at me threateningly.

"'Nothing!" I said quickly. "But I need to know what sort of thing it is. Because I have to fix the price."

"'Price?" they repeated.

'"Everything has a price. Sending something by train costs money."

'"Oh, yes," they said. "And who does the money go to? You, I suppose?"

'"Not me," I said hastily. "It goes to the government."

'"It goes to Ali Maher, I'll bet!" said one of them.

'"No, no," I said. "It goes to the government. To pay for the railway." They spoke among themselves.

'"Tell us how much it is," they said at last.

'"That depends on what sort of thing it is," I said. "Which is what I asked you. Is it, for example, a piece of furniture – a table, say?"

'"Table? Are you mocking us? Anyone can see it's not a table!"

'"I give you that as an example. What sort of thing is it? What class of thing? Is it, for instance, a present?" They laughed.

'"Yes, yes," they said. "It is a present."

'"Right then," I said, and told them how much it was to cost. They looked blue.

'"That is a lot of money!" they said.

'"It is the normal price," I said. "The one the government determines."

'"And what is the cut you get?" they asked. I told you, Effendis, they were ignorant men.

'"Without the money," I said, "it does not travel."

'Well, they put their heads together, and there was much counting of *milliemes*. But in the end they found what was required. So I made out the ticket and gave it them. "This is to say that you have given me the money, lest anyone say you haven't."

'"It would be a bad thing for them if they tried that!" one of them said.

'"Keep the ticket," I said. "Then there can be no dispute."

'"And now it can go?" they asked.

'"Now it can go," I confirmed.

'"What a to-do about a small thing!" they said.

'And then they went away and I was glad. To tell the truth, I did not greatly care for them.'

Denderah station was just a place where the train stopped
to take in water for the engine. Its most conspicuous feature
was the water tower that Leila had described. There was no
platform and only the single building where the clerk presided.
Apart from the Inglesi who came to view the temple, he said,
there were few passengers.

'And the village?' asked Owen.

The clerk pointed over the long *halfeh* grass to some doum
palms in the distance.

'So,' said Owen, 'you are Mustapha the basket maker?'

Mustapha looked up, startled, from the reeds he was
holding between his toes. 'I am, indeed, Mustapha,' he said
uneasily.

Owen crouched down to one side of him, a little to his front.
Mahmoud had taken up a similar position on the other side.

'Tell us, Mustapha: are you a family man?'

'God has blessed me,' Mustapha said warily.

'With children? How many?'

'Five,' said the basket maker, not without pride.

'That is blessed indeed. And are they still with you?'

'Three are.'

'And the other two?'

'Have gone away,' said the basket maker, hesitating.

'Oh, indeed? How so?'

There was a pause.

'They married,' the basket maker said, after a moment.

'Both of them?'

'Both.'

'How old were they?'

'Thirteen.'

'Both of them?'

'The oldest was thirteen,' said the basket maker unwillingly.

'And the youngest?'

'Nine.'

'Nine. That is young to get married.'

'She was ready for it.'

'Shame on you, Mustapha!' said a woman's voice from the
back of the crowd that had gathered.

'Peace, woman!' said the basket maker angrily. 'She wished it. When her sister went, she wanted to go, too.'

'Ah, but not into marriage,' said Owen.

'A man offered for her, and she was willing!'

'Ah, yes, but what did he offer?'

'A good home. Well provided.'

'Better than yours, perhaps? Especially since you took a new wife.'

'He knows all!' someone called out.

'What if he does?' said the basket maker angrily. 'There is no law against taking another wife.'

'There is against selling a child, though,' said Mahmoud.

'She went to a good home! She wanted it.'

'Whose home?'

'A man's. I do not know his name.'

'You sold your daughter to a man and you do not know his name?'

'I did *not* sell her.'

'How much did he give you?'

The basket maker rose to his feet furiously. 'I shall not listen!'

'You will,' said Mahmoud. 'Sit down!'

The basket maker hesitated, then sat down. 'Who are you?' he whispered.

'The Parquet,' said Mahmoud. 'And this is the Mamur Zapt.'

Owen was never sure how well the title was known outside Cairo, but there was a little ripple of astonishment in the crowd that had gathered. Owen and Mahmoud didn't mind the crowd. Sometimes it had its advantages.

'What do you want from us?' said Mustapha sullenly.

'The truth. What is the name of the man you sold her to?'

'I . . . I do not know. I have told you!'

Mustapha shook his head unhappily.

'You don't know? Or you won't tell?'

'I don't know.'

'Your daughter goes to a house and you don't know where it is?'

'A long way away,' muttered the basket maker.

'Ah, there I believe you,' said Mahmoud.

'What is this?' Mustapha broke out angrily. 'Why do you question me? She wished to get married; a man made a good offer – what is wrong with that?'

'And you cannot tell me the name of the man, nor the place of his home? Good offer, indeed! Would her mother have thought so? Her true mother?'

'When you have five children, you cannot do as well for them as you would like. She knew she would have to marry. In our village all the children know that. She had known that for a long time.'

'Long enough to make ready a bride box?'

'The offer came sooner than I had expected.'

'So she didn't have a bride box? Unlike her sister?'

'Her sister had a bride box, certainly. She had more time to prepare one.'

'Yes,' said Mahmoud. 'I have seen it.'

There was a stir of amazement in the crowd.

A woman pushed through the people. She was poorly dressed and didn't wear a veil. Her cheeks were cut with tribal marks and her hands were dyed with henna. She was shouting angrily, 'What is this? What is this? What are you doing with my man?'

'Asking questions,' said Mahmoud. 'Which have to be answered.'

'What questions?'

'About your daughters. Your new daughters. The ones who were in your husband's house when you came but are not there now.'

'Well, what of it?' the woman said, more warily. 'They have gone away, that is all. Who asks these questions?'

'The police,' said someone in the crowd.

'The police? Hah!' the woman scoffed. 'What do I care about the police?'

'The police from Cairo.'

The woman put her hand over her mouth and stood for a moment looking uncertainly around her. Then she sat down on the ground beside her husband.

'Is there an *omda*?' asked Mahmoud, referring to a village headman.

'Yes, Effendi.'

'Fetch him.'

It took a little time. Meanwhile, Owen and Mahmoud sat patiently there on the ground, the crowd growing all the time. The people sat there quietly, but Owen knew they were taking everything in. That could be helpful later, if only as a check on what the basket maker had said. In a village like this everyone knew everything. What was perhaps more to the point, they know what was *not* being said.

At last a man came pushing through the crowd. He looked worried. 'Effendis?'

'Salaam Aleikhum,' said Owen and Mahmoud together, politely.

'And to you, Salaam!' returned the omda.

'I am from the Parquet,' said Mahmoud, 'and this is the Mamur Zapt.'

There was no doubt about the Mamur Zapt being known to the omda. He became tense. 'You come from Cairo?' he said. 'It is a long way.'

'Even there we hear of things. We hear, for example, that children have gone missing from your village.'

The omda went still. 'One of them went to get married,' he said, after a moment.

'So it is said. And the other?'

'I do not know.'

'The one who went to get married: do you know the name of the man to whom she was to be married or the place of her new home? No? Is that the way things are done in Denderah?'

The omda was silent for a moment. 'It is the way they were done on this occasion,' he said quietly. 'But not the way they should have been done. I knew nothing about it until after she was gone.'

'Did you not make enquiries?'

'We wondered, and asked. But her father said that he had received a good offer and that the matter had to be closed quickly.'

'Without any celebration?'

'There would be celebrations, her father told us. But they could be elsewhere.'

'How could you be sure she was to be wed?'

'She took her bride box, Effendi.'

'And so you thought that . . .?'

'What else could it mean?'

'I have seen the bride box,' said Mahmoud. 'But not the things that she put in it. Have you seen them?'

'No, Effendi!' said the omda, shocked. 'How could we?'

'I think they may have been tipped out and left. In which case they must be lying around somewhere. Perhaps not far from the village. And if they were left like that, some of them may have been found and brought back here. Have they been?'

The omda, still shocked, turned to the villagers. 'Have they?' he asked.

There was a mutter of denial.

'Look for them,' said Mahmoud. 'And if you find them, bring them to me. No one will be punished just for having these things, but I need to know about them.'

'They were Soraya's things!' a woman said indignantly. 'She was making ready for her wedding. They should not have been treated like that!'

'Where is Soraya?' someone asked.

Owen and Mahmoud exchanged glances. Owen nodded.

'She is dead,' said Mahmoud.

Mustapha's new wife collapsed, weeping. Mustapha bowed his head to the ground and seemed to be trying to push his face into the sand. Some women at the back of the crowd began to wail.

There was no lock-up in the village. There was no constable, either. Mahmoud told Mustapha and his wife to stay in their house and made the omda responsible for seeing to it. Then he and Owen walked over to the village well and sat down on the little mud-brick wall that was built around it. People would come to them, they knew; but it would take time.

First, the omda himself came. 'Would Your Excellencies like tea?' he said anxiously. 'Or perhaps beer?'

'No beer, thank you,' said Mahmoud.

Owen shook his head. 'Tea would be welcome,' he said.

Shortly afterwards a woman brought them tea, the bitter, black tea of the fellahin, on a wicker work tray. Afterwards she continued to stand there.

'Yes?'

'The body needs seeing to, Effendi,' she said.

It was a rule that the body should be buried the day the person died.

'That cannot be in this case,' said Mahmoud. 'The body is in Cairo. It is being seen to.'

'It should be seen to by those that knew her,' said the woman.

'That cannot be.'

The woman stood for a while, then accepted it. 'And what of Leila?' she asked.

'Leila is in Cairo, too,' said Owen. 'She is well and in safe hands.'

'God be praised!'

'Perform such rites as you can,' said Mahmoud.

The woman nodded and went away and shortly afterwards the wailing rose in volume. It sounded as if all the women of the village were taking part – and perhaps they were.

The wailing continued all night and was still going on when they woke up the next morning. They had been taken to a house to spend the night and given food. In the morning when they went out the women were already busy drawing up water from the well.

Owen and Mahmoud went and stood by them.

'Is it true, Effendi, what you said about Leila?' one of them asked quietly.

'It is true, yes.'

'*Inshallah!* God be praised!'

'How did it come about that she was allowed to go? What sort of village is this?'

'No one knew, Effendi. It was all done by the father and he told no one else. We had heard that slavers were in the district but no one had seen them. Mustapha must have sought them out.'

'And Soraya? The same?'

'Perhaps, Effendi. I do not know. She had disappeared some days before. Again in the night, and silently. Again it was her father's doing. But, Effendi . . .'

'Yes?'

'The cases are not the same. Soraya must have thought she was going to be wed, for she took her bride box with her. Perhaps her father had told her some story.'

'And then sold her to the slavers?'

'Perhaps. But . . .'

'Yes?'

'Would the slavers have killed a pretty girl? Surely not! They would have kept her alive and sold her. She would have fetched a good price.'

'I thought the slavers had gone from Egypt,' Mahmoud said. 'How comes it that they are here?'

'I don't know. I had thought those days were over, too. I remember when I was a child – well, we would see the slaving caravans sometimes. And then we would run indoors and our mothers would hide us. And they would say to their husbands: "If my child goes, you will not wake up tomorrow!" I remember my own mother saying that. Not that my father would have sold us.' The woman laughed, tenderly. 'He wouldn't have sold me for the world. But some men would. Well, that was long ago! Those days are past.'

'They should be,' said Mahmoud. 'How comes it that they are not?'

'It is the Pashas!' said the woman bitterly. 'There is one law for the rich and another for the poor. And what makes the law is money.'

Owen and Mahmoud continued to sit on at the well. They both knew that it was the way you had to do business in an Egyptian village. It was no good going round and questioning as you might in Cairo. In the village you had to wait for them to come to you. And there was a lot of thinking to be done before that would happen.

Although they were in the shade of the palms, the heat increased steadily. The centre of the village was now almost deserted. And yet there was something agreeable about just sitting there dozing. The doves gurgled in the palm trees, there was the occasional bray of a donkey and always, in the background, the continual creak of the water wheel by the river. It was peaceful, and even Mahmoud, with all the restlessness of a city dweller, succumbed to the effect.

At last the omda came up again and hovered uneasily. 'What is it that Your Excellencies wish to know, Effendis?' he asked anxiously.

'About the slavers,' said Owen.

'If I could tell you, I would, Effendi, but there is little to tell. We heard that they were in the area and I couldn't believe it. They have not been here since my father's time. But so it was whispered. And the whispers grew. "How can this be?" I asked. But no one could answer me. "Keep the children indoors!" I said. And it was done. Except that Mustapha must have seen his chance and went out to seek them. Effendi, I cannot understand such evil! But this is a poor village and when men are in need they do evil things.'

'Where did they come from?' asked Owen. 'The slavers?'

'The Sudan, I think. It is not far from here, at a camel ride. And the border is uncertain.'

'And where do they go to?'

'No one knows, Effendi, but surely it must be to the coast. People are not bought and sold in Egypt these days. Not openly.'

'To the coast, then. And where on the coast?'

'There are ports in the Sudan.'

'If there were whispers when they came, there will be whispers when they go. I would like to hear those whispers.'

'You shall, Effendi.'

The object of Mahmoud's inquiries was not the same as that of Owen's. Although Mahmoud was just as concerned as Owen about the slave issue – possibly more, since he took it personally as an affront to Egypt and yet more evidence of the country falling short of his ideals – what he was here for was to find out what had happened to Soraya. And, he thought, he was making progress. The clerk at the railway halt would surely be able to identify the men who had brought the box to the station. He might be unwilling to but he would be able to.

And surely, thought Mahmoud, he knew enough now to be able to find the men. They had said themselves that they were the Pasha's men. They had spoken of 'our' Pasha and had even given his name. It was no surprise: Ali Maher, whom he had already been to see. And who had said that he had no connection with Denderah. While all the time he had an estate here.

Clearly, what he would have to do now was to go to the estate. He would take the clerk with him to identify the men. Then he would arrest the men, bring them back to Denderah and then get on the next train to Cairo. It was all straightforward.

Except . . .

Except that nothing in Egypt was quite straightforward. How, for instance, was he going to get to the estate? It was only a few miles out of Denderah, but how was he going to cross those few miles? In Cairo (ah, Cairo!) it would have been simple. He would have hopped on the train or taken a cab. A horse-drawn cab, admittedly, but there would have been no difficulty in finding one. Just outside his office there was a row of them.

Here, however, in benighted Upper Egypt there weren't any. Nor any trains, either. So what was he to do? Walk? Seven miles across the desert? No, thank you! Horse, then? There would be horses here, although so far he had not seen any. But Mahmoud, every inch an urban Cairene, had never ridden a horse and wasn't sure he knew quite how to manage one. They were a long way up. Not as high as a camel – but that was definitely out of the question! Discreet enquiries confirmed what he had feared: he would have to go by donkey.

Fortunately, it was easy to hire one. In fact, he hired two, one for himself, and one for the clerk, who was possibly even less enthusiastic about the proposal than he was.

'But, Effendi, my duties at the station . . .'

'Find someone to stand in for you.'

'But . . .'

But in the end a substitute was found – the clerk's brother.

Jobs in Egypt were best kept in the family. The brother was buoyant about it, the clerk less so.

Owen continued to sit by the well. It was about midway through the morning that a boy who introduced himself as Selim came up to him. He was holding a scarf in his hands.

'This was Soraya's,' he said simply.

He had found it, he said, out beyond the doum trees, beyond the temple, towards the river. There were other things there, too. He had left them there that Owen might see them.

'Let us go, then,' said Owen.

The things were lying on the sand, apparently thrown out casually, as if the box had simply been tipped out; as if the box was what was wanted and the contents of no more importance than the girl who had owned them. They were humble things – a shawl, slippers, a cotton dress. But the shawl and the dress had been lovingly embroidered. Even the beads on the slippers had been carefully sewn on. He looked at them carefully. They were glass beads; not trocchee shells.

The boy was still holding the scarf. 'This I gave to Soraya,' he said quietly.

'You gave it to her? As a present?'

The boy nodded.

'Was there an understanding between you?'

The boy hesitated. 'An understanding only. And no one knew. There could not be an agreement. We were too young. And her father, we knew, would not have it. He wanted someone who was older and in a position to give more. But she said she would wait.'

'So you were surprised when you learned that she had not waited?'

'I could not believe it! To do it without a word! But then her father told me she had taken her bride box with her and I saw that it was so. And I went off by myself into the desert and said that she was faithless. But, Effendi . . .'

'Yes?'

'I do not believe that. I have gone over it in my mind again and again, and still I do not believe it. It was a trick, a trick of her greedy father. But, Effendi, even if what he had said was true, and she had gone to another, I would not have minded as much as I do *this*. That she should have gone and not just from me but from . . . *life* . . .'

The tears were streaming down his face.

'Effendi, if ever I find out who did this terrible thing, I will kill him!'

The women had finished, for the moment, their filling of buckets and the little square of the town had reverted to its normal doze. In the doum palms the doves, too, had subsided. Only a steady gurgling, almost a purr, emerged from their throats.

The omda came out of one of the houses, followed by a group of men. The men scattered, but not so far that they could not watch proceedings, leaving the omda alone to come across to Owen.

'Effendi . . .'

'Yes?'

'We have spoken with Mustapha.'

'Good!'

'He is willing to confess all.'

'You have done well.'

'It is not so much our doing but his wife's. She could not sleep, she said, for thinking about the consequences of his foolishness. And to persist with it! There was no standing out against the mighty, she insisted. The police, especially around here, are nothing – but the Khedive is another matter. In the end he will have what he wills, and he has strong arms. Not for nothing does the Mamur Zapt come down to Denderah. His eye is on all things, even on what we do with our daughters. It is useless to try to deceive him. Or to deny him. Either you answer his questions here, she told him, or you answer them in jail.'

'Those are words of wisdom,' said Owen.

'Mustapha did not think so at first. He said: "I shall not answer even though they put me in jail." And his wife said: "Not at first, perhaps; but as the years go by? I don't want to see you rot in jail while I wait outside the door. You have done wrong. Admit it, and take your punishment. And then it will be all over and done with and we can get on with our lives again."

'And we told him,' said the omda, 'that what she said was wisdom. But still he wouldn't have it. "Must I suffer, just for daughters?" he said.

"'I was a daughter once," she said.

"'You were with me in this," he told her.

"'I was wrong," she said, "and will go to the Mamur Zapt and tell him so."

"'He will have you whipped," said Mustapha.

"'He won't," she said. "'He will put me in jail. Nor will he whip you if you go to him."

"'He will put me in jail," said Mustapha, "which is worse."

"'You will go to jail anyway," we told him. "And justly so. Wipe the slate clean before you go, and then at least we will be able to remember you without shrinking."'

'So now he will speak?' said Owen.

'Yes, Effendi.'

'You have done well.'

He got up from the wall.

'Show me his house.'

He had forgotten how deep the poverty of rural Egypt was. The house was bare. There was not even a bed, just some shawls thrown down casually in a corner. There was no table. Just a rough native chest in which things were stored. There was a brazier for a fire to cook on, a sack of durra. The wife would prepare the meal outside. The children would eat, and naturally sleep, outside. How had Soraya succeeded in preparing the things for her box? Everything here was a wrestle with life.

The house was dark and low. There was only the single room. If Mustapha had been just that little bit wealthier he would have had a water buffalo, which would probably have shared the house with them. In the yard outside there were one or two hens and a pile of the basket maker's raw materials.

The omda had entered the house with him, followed by a small crowd of people.

'Do you wish the elders to stay?' asked Owen. If they did, they could act as witnesses.

Mustapha made a gesture of indifference.

'Right, then, stay,' said Owen, 'that you may see that what is done is justice.'

Mustapha, prompted by his wife, ran through what he had told Owen already. In the case of Leila there was little to add. He had heard that there were slavers in the district and one evening, when he had been drinking – and had, he said, been provoked by his daughters – had decided to put an end to it and at the same time to turn them to profit.

'And you urged me!' he said, turning to his wife.

'I did. It had become impossible to live with them. Particularly Soraya.'

The sale of Leila had gone through without difficulty. He had gone to see the chief slaver and the deal had been struck at once.

'One moment,' said Owen, 'the chief slaver. Was that the white man?'

'No. He stood mostly to one side. There was an Egyptian in charge at the caravan.'

And that, as far as Leila was concerned, was about it. Money had changed hands, Leila had been passed over and, as far as Mustapha knew, had joined the other children in the caravan.

'And Soraya?'

This had been less straightforward. Yes, the slaver had wanted her. But not for himself. He already seemed to have known about her because it was he who had raised the question of her sale to Mustapha. He seemed to be acting on behalf of someone else, someone who had seen Soraya and taken a fancy to her. He had asked the slaver to act as intermediary and would pass her back to the slaver when he had finished, so that the slaver would be doubly in wealth.

For the buyer was prepared to pay quite a lot for Soraya. Mustapha had by chance overheard the sum the slaver was expecting and it was considerable. It had quite taken Mustapha's breath away. The size of the sum was what had made Mustapha think that the buyer must have more in mind

than the purchase of a mere slave. He had asked the slaver
if she should bring her bride box. The slaver had laughed and
said: 'Why not?'

So when he had told Soraya to come with him, he had told
her to bring her bride box. And Soraya had said: 'Why should
I bring my bride box when I am not to be wed?' And he
had said: 'Don't be so sure of that!' And Soraya had said she
did not want to marry a man she knew nothing of. And
Mustapha had lost patience with her, thinking that this was
yet more of her difficult behaviour. And he had said all that
she needed to know was that he was rich. 'What if he were a
Pasha?' he had said. And Soraya had been intrigued and had
agreed to at least meet him.

'But I shall not wed him if I don't think him worthy!'
she had said. And Mustapha had lost his temper and said
that if she went on like this, no one would want her. And
she had said she knew someone who would. And that had
made Mustapha even angrier, for he knew who she was
thinking of.

'It was Selim, Effendi, a poor boy from the village, worth
nothing, and who never will be worth anything. Worthless
entirely. So I told her to put him out of her mind and at least
see what else was on offer. Which she agreed to do. And I
was confident, Effendi, that when she saw that he was a rich
man she would have some sense. And so I sent her bride box
with her.'

'Tell me about the slaver.'

'He was not from these parts.'

'What part was he from?'

Mustapha hesitated. 'I do not know. The Sudan, I think.'

'What was he called? Come, you must have known what
he was called.'

'Abdulla,' Mustapha said reluctantly.

'The rest of his name?'

'Sardawi.'

'Abdulla Sardawi. That is how he is known, yes?'

'Yes,' said Mustapha.

'And you think he comes from the Sudan. Why do you
think he comes from the Sudan?'

'My wife was a Sudani,' said Mustapha. 'My first wife.'

'Ah!' said Owen. 'That explains it.'

'Explains . . .?'

'Your first wife, was she a dark Sudani? Is that how Leila comes to be so dark?'

'She took after her mother.'

'And Soraya?'

'She was less dark. She took after her mother, too, but more after me.'

'She was lighter in colour?'

'The mother was light but there was darkness in her. Her blood was mixed.'

'She was the beautiful one,' said his second wife, from the hall.

'And therefore most likely to make a good marriage?' asked Owen.

'That was what I thought. And hoped.'

'But looks are not all,' said his current wife. 'She had the devil in her.'

'She was older,' said Owen, 'and there was always going to be trouble between you two.'

'That is so,' the woman agreed. 'Nevertheless, I would not have dealt with her harshly if she had not been so difficult.'

'We were afraid that Leila would grow up like her,' said Mustapha. 'So we thought it best to get rid of them both. The others are more amenable.'

'Being younger,' his wife explained. 'I would not have you think that I am always a bad mother. I would have brought them up to be dutiful.'

'A man must have a peaceful home,' said Mustapha. 'He cannot do with discord in the family.'

'Always trouble,' said his wife. 'Always. There was always trouble with that girl.'

'Soraya?' said Owen.

'Soraya, yes. So it was a blessing when she was noticed.'

'By the slave trader?'

'No, no, not by the slaver. She was noticed first, and then Abdulla was asked to see what he could do.'

'Who was this person who first noticed her?'

'I do not know.'

'You do not know?'

'I know only that Abdulla came on his behalf.'

'Without telling you the man's name?' said Owen incredulously.

'He said it didn't matter.'

'So you knew it was not a question of marriage?'

'Be careful, Mustapha!' counselled the wife, from beside the wall.

'I hoped it *would* become a question of marriage,' said Mustapha, turning to her. 'She is a beautiful girl. Was it not likely that someone should ask after her?'

'Asking after her is one thing,' said Owen. 'This is another.'

'It could have led to a proposal. That is what I hoped.'

'You hoped, even though you knew it was a slaver who asked?' said Owen sceptically.

'I hoped, yes!' said Mustapha defensively. 'There is nothing wrong with hoping, is there, and was it not likely that when the asker had seen her more closely, he would wish it to be? That is what I reasoned. And so I bade her take her bride box with her.'

# FOUR

They set off early, when the sun was poking up above the horizon, huge and blood-red, like an enormous orange. It shot up with what seemed to Mahmoud, who was not one for sunrises, incredible speed. The redness on the sand disappeared and was replaced by a soothing grey, which soon become less soothing – indeed, so bright and glaring that it hurt the eyes. The morning, which had been pleasantly cool, warmed up. The heat began to press down on his shoulders. Soon after, the first drops of sweat started to fall on the patient neck of the donkey, and at about the same time he began to discover new muscles in his thighs and new sources of pain.

After a while, he realized that the sand had given way to cultivated fields of durra. The green was more soothing on the eye. But then the durra grew taller and he was soon riding through great banks of it, which trapped the heat and attracted the insects. They came in swarms and lay black on the neck of the donkey, on the thighs of his trousers and on his arms. He had to keep brushing them from his face. It was sheer misery. As he had known it would be!

He told himself it was only for a short time, that he would arrest the men and then get back to Cairo. And never, never leave Cairo again! Much less return to Upper Egypt.

The clerk urged his donkey up alongside Mahmoud.

'Effendi, they will kill me!'

'No, they won't.

'They will see my face and know me.'

'Cover your face, then.'

'They will still know me,' said the clerk despondently.

'I will find a way that you can see and not be seen.'

Happier, but not happy, the clerk fell back.

\* \* \*

Ahead of him, through the sand, he saw a large white house.

He stopped and told the clerk to stay out of sight. Then he went on. There was a bell-rope by the door. He pulled. After some minutes a man came to the door.

'The Pasha? He's not here.'

'Very well, then. Take me to the one in charge.'

The servant slipped away and sometime later another man appeared. He looked at Mahmoud suspiciously and disdainfully.

'The Pasha is not at home.'

'No? That is a pity, for there are questions I have to put to him.'

'You will have to put them in Cairo, then.'

Mahmoud was irked. This was no way to receive a stranger. And most unusual.

'Perhaps you can help me.'

'I don't think so.'

Mahmoud, tired after his long ride, boiled over. 'This is the Parquet. I come on the Khedive's business. Summon all the servants!'

The man hesitated. 'The Pasha . . .'

'I am here in the Pasha's interest. I have spoken with the Pasha.'

'They are in the fields . . .'

'Fetch them from the fields, then.'

'It will take some time.'

'I will wait. But I do not propose to wait long. If they are not here shortly I will put you in the caracol.'

The man flinched. 'They will be here,' he said.

'In the yard. I want them in the yard.'

'In the yard,' repeated the man.

He did not offer to take Mahmoud into the house and Mahmoud was annoyed about this, too. It was rank discourtesy.

After some time a man came and took his donkey. Mahmoud followed him round the side of the house into a large yard where there was a drinking trough. The donkey bent to it greedily.

Another servant, an older man, came out of the house bringing a jug of lemonade.

'It is a hot day, Effendi,' he said. 'Take some refreshment.'

'Thank you,' said Mahmoud. 'I had begun to think that manners had been forgotten in the south.'

'Don't bother about him,' the man said, jerking his head after his departed superior. 'He's always like that. Is it true you wish to speak to the men?'

Mahmoud nodded.

'They won't be sorry if it means that they can finish earlier. What was it that you wished to see them about?'

Mahmoud considered; then, thinking there was nothing to be lost, said: 'It concerns a bride box.'

'A bride box!'

'One that was put on the train.'

'Effendi, I think you must be mistaken. There are no bride boxes here. Nor are there likely to be.' He stopped short, as if he had been about to say something he shouldn't. 'There are no young girls here of the right age,' he said. But that was not, Mahmoud was sure, what he had been going to say. 'Why a bride box, Effendi?' he asked.

'One that was put on the train. And sent to the Pasha.'

'Ah. Now I understand. But, Effendi, you are still mistaken. No bride box has been sent from here. I would have known if there had been.'

'The men who put it on the train said they were from here.'

The servant shook his head. 'Effendi, I still find that hard to understand. Men do not come and go from here just as they wish. It means a day out of the fields and Ismail would not let that happen.'

'Ismail is the man in charge?'

'You have seen what he is like.'

'Nevertheless, that is what the men said. They even gave the Pasha's name, Ali Maher.'

'Ali Maher is certainly the Pasha here. But why, Effendi, would he be sending a box to himself? In Cairo?'

'That is what I am trying to find out.'

'Perhaps he intends to get married again? And his eye has

alighted on some girl? But if that is so, I do not know of it. And surely I would . . .'

'There are questions to be asked,' said Mahmoud.

'Evidently,' said the servant, still shaking his head.

Men began to assemble in the yard. Mahmoud went for a walk around the outhouses. There were quite a few of them. The estate was obviously a large one.

In one of the buildings stood some carts, used for bringing in the durra. One had a half-awning which covered most of the cart. It would do.

He went back round the house to where he had left the clerk. He found him sitting in the shade beneath a bush.

'Come with me,' he said and then, choosing his moment when there was no one to see, led him round to the cart with the half-awning and told him to get inside. Part of the awning was rolled back and the clerk could hide under it.

Mahmoud went back into the yard. 'Are the men all here?' he asked.

Ismail nodded sourly.

'Right, I will speak to them.'

He looked at the men. There were about twenty of them, all in short galabeyas, showing their arms and legs burnt black by the sun. 'I need something to stand on.'

He beckoned to two of the men and then went into the outhouse. 'This one will do,' he said.

The men took the cart with the half-awning and the clerk round into the yard.

Mahmoud climbed up on to the cart. 'Which of you has been to the station at Denderah in the past fortnight?'

They looked at him blankly.

Mahmoud sighed and made them file past him. 'Can you see them?' he whispered to the clerk.

'Effendi, I can see them,' the clerk whispered back. 'But the men who came to the station are not amongst them!'

'Look once more!'

He made the men file past again, but with the same result. 'Effendi, I do not see them,' said the clerk worriedly. 'I really don't!'

'Are all the men here?' Mahmoud asked Ismail.

'They are all here, Effendi.'

Mahmoud got down from the cart and walked over to the men. 'Are you all here?' he asked. 'No one is missing?'

The men looked at each other. 'No one is missing, Effendi. We are all here.'

Mahmoud was nonplussed. He had counted on the clerk being able to identify them. He made them file past once more but again drew a blank. He knew he would have to let them go.

He saw Ismail looking at him with an air of triumph, and made one last attempt. 'None of you has been to Denderah recently?'

They looked at him blankly.

'It concerns a bride box,' he said.

There was a flicker of interest.

'A bride box which was taken to the station in Denderah and put on the train.'

He was losing them. Bride boxes were within their experience; trains, however . . .

'And sent to the Pasha,' he tried desperately.

That was interesting. It was even funny. A bride box! For the Pasha!

But it didn't register particularly with the men as it should have.

'They can go now?' asked Ismail, almost insolently.

Mahmoud made one last try. 'Have any of you a bride box in your house?'

One or two nodded.

'And still have? None have been sent away lately?'

They shook their heads.

'Effendi,' said Ismail, 'there is another consideration. To take a bride box to the station at Denderah would require a cart. A cart could come only from here and no cart could be moved without my permission. My permission has not been given. Nor has it been sought. You are asking at the wrong place; asking the wrong people.'

Mahmoud had to let them go. He got four of them to take the cart he had borrowed back to the outhouse. The men went away and shortly afterwards he saw the clerk, standing beside the barn, much relieved. He left the yard behind some women returning to the kitchen who had been interested in the spectacle and could hear them talking.

'Bride box!' one of them sighed. 'I had a bride box once. Ah, those were the days!'

'Mine was green and orange,' said another woman wistfully. 'And blue for the sky.'

'Mine had birds.'

'And mine had fish.'

'I had a bird *catching* a fish!'

'Beautiful!'

'Ah, those were the days.'

The party broke up.

'Are you coming in?'

'No, I've got to get back to the other house.'

'Other house?' Mahmoud, overhearing, asked them.

They turned to look at him.

'Yes, the other house.'

'What house is this?'

'It is where the Pasha's wife lives now that she does not live with him.'

'Another house? Does she have servants?'

'Of course.'

'Servants of her own? They would not have been with the others?'

'You asked only for men on the estate.'

'Why was I not told?' said Mahmoud furiously.

He knew, really. This was Ismail's revenge.

'There is this one, which the Pasha uses when he is here. The other is for his wife.'

'And the son.'

'There is a son?'

'In a manner of speaking.'

There was a ripple of amusement.

'*She*'s the master there!' someone said.

Behind the temple were the mountains, pink and as if floating in the air, with satiny sand drifts heaped in the rifts in the rock and lines of soft blue shadow in the more remote crevices. Where the mountain fell back a long vista of desert was revealed.

As Owen approached, by a raised fragmented causeway which linked the temple with some paint down by the river, he found himself in a kind of derelict area, with low half-opened mounds, broken bits of sculptural capitals and mutilated statues buried in tall clumps of rank grass: but also little damaged buildings which might once have been workshops and a vast number of semi-subterranean tanks with black tarry patches inside them which showed that once they had contained nitre.

Egypt is the land of nitre. The Nile mud is impregnated with it. It lies in talc-like flakes upon the rocks, upon the fallen statues. The nitre has been worked for centuries. It is washed and crystallized in the tanks and made workable. In the days of the Ottomans it began to be used for gunpowder.

He stood for a moment in front of the temple, looking up at the great, heavy bulk of stonework. And then he had a moment of shock, for it appeared to be moving! He looked again and saw that it was a swarm of bees, flooding out from crevices in the stonework.

He went into the temple. In the half-light he saw great columns stretching away into the distance. He was in a huge hall, with a line of columns on either side. As his eyes grew used to the darkness he saw that their tops were carved into images of birds: hawks, ibises, bird-faced humans, the traditional figures of the old gods. Here and there was a representation of a cow with horns.

Between the columns, on the roof, were paintings. The paintings were of the holy scarab beetle and some curious winged globes. Looking at them more closely he saw that they were in patterns. Gradually he realized that the patterns were astronomical. He was looking at the famous signs of the Zodiac: Leila's 'marks of the giants'.

'So this is where you came with Soraya,' he said to Selim, whom he had brought with him.

Selim shrugged. 'It was a place to go, where we would not be seen,' he said.

'And Leila came, too?'

'She stood outside to warn us if anyone should be coming. She wouldn't go in. She said it was a bad place and smelt of the dead. However, she agreed to keep watch for us.'

'And did anyone come?'

'Once, as I told you. One day the slaver came.'

'How did you know he was the slaver?'

Selim shrugged. 'They had spoken of him in the village. I knew he was the man.'

'What sort of man was he?'

'A Sudani.'

'You are sure?'

'I am sure. I heard him speak.'

'This was at the temple?'

'Yes.'

'You heard them speaking together?'

'Yes, we were hiding behind the pillars. They had come suddenly and Leila had had no time to warn us.'

'So you heard what they were saying?'

'A little, yes. We dared not go too close.'

'What were they talking about?'

'There was talk of deliveries.'

'Slaves?'

'I do not think so. For they spoke of a consignment and where it could be stored. The slaver said that the temple was a good place because it was big and had many rooms, in some of which, deep inside, things could be stowed and no one would find them. People were afraid of the temple and did not like to go in. The white man said that it sounded ideal, and the slaver said that he would show him a place. Then they both went off deeper into the temple and Soraya said we should go now that there was the chance. Particularly as Leila was sure she had been seen.'

'So you went and did not see the place they had gone to?'

'No, but later I went back on my own, when there was no one there. I did not like going; I was afraid I would lose my way and never get out. Still, I went.'

'And did you find the place?'

'Yes, I am almost sure. It was in a room at the back of the

temple. It was off another one so well concealed that unless you knew it was there and where to look, you would not find it. But I had a torch with me and saw marks in the sand where they had been, and I followed the marks. And when I got there I knew it was the place because I found an old box and in it I found a shell.'

'A trocchee shell?'

'No, no. A gun shell. A bullet. One they use in rifles.'

'That is very interesting. Could you show it to me?'

'I have it at home.'

'I would like to see it. And perhaps the place where it was left.'

When they came out again into the sunlight Owen's eye was caught by a flash from one of the nitre tanks. For a moment he thought there must be some water in it, but then he realized it must be from the tar. Odd, he thought, that the connection between the temple and warfare should be so long-standing and still continuing.

Now that he had emerged victorious, Ismail, the head of the Pasha's household, was prepared to be conciliatory. He sent a servant with them to show them off the estate. They went by a different route from the one they had come by.

'It is quicker,' said the servant.

The path led through a field of *berseem*, food stuff for the animals of the household, and then through thin acacia shrub. Through the scrub they occasionally caught a glimpse of the Nile. Then they turned away and headed inland. A road forked off, and on it a dead donkey was lying, buzzing with flies.

'It is to attract the jackals,' said the servant. 'For the master to shoot.'

'The master? He is here, then?'

'The young master.'

'Ah, the son.'

'The son, yes. He stays with his mother.'

'And he shoots jackals?'

'What else is there for him to do?'

The servant stopped when they got to the fork. 'Keep on this way,' he said, 'and it will take you back to Denderah.'

'And the other path?'

'Leads you to the other house.'

'Where the Pasha's lady lives?'

'That is so, yes.'

The servant turned back and they continued on their way.

For only a little way. Then they stopped, and after a moment or two turned back.

'What are we doing?' said the clerk. 'That is the way to Denderah!'

'We will go somewhere else first.'

This arm of the fork was more overgrown and they had to push past scrub branches which dangled across the path.

There was the sudden crack of a rifle shot and a branch in front of them jumped suddenly. The clerk hurled himself to the ground.

Mahmoud stepped back behind a tree. 'Stop shooting!' he shouted. 'There are people here!'

There was no reply. And then a man pushed out of the bushes ahead of them. 'Frightfully sorry!' he said, speaking in English, not in Arabic. He came forward, one hand held up before him apologetically.

He was an Egyptian, however, not English, a man in his mid-twenties. His hair was already beginning to recede, leaving the top front of his head bald and shiny, and there seemed something odd about him.

He was immaculately dressed in a newly laundered white shirt and newly pressed trousers. 'Frightfully sorry!' he repeated. 'I didn't know you were there. We don't get many visitors. And, anyway,' he said in a puzzled voice, 'I don't know how I came to miss it! I don't usually. I think I may have caught a glimpse of you out of the corner of my eye and been distracted. Yes, that would be it! I don't see how I could have missed it otherwise. I saw it quite clearly. A big fat one perched on a bough. An easy shot. Frightfully sorry! I hope you're all right?'

'No damage done,' said Mahmoud.

'Oh, good!' He looked down at the clerk still lying on the ground. 'And what about you?'

The clerk rose sheepishly.

'You *look* all right. Not a scratch, as far as I can see. But, I say, you must come back into the house! Have a drink or something.'

He went up to the door, which had remained closed, and hammered on it. 'Yussef! Osman! Wake up!'

The door opened slowly.

'Come on, Yussef, it's only me. Except that I've brought some visitors. This is . . .?'

'Mahmoud el Zaki. The Parquet.'

'Mr el Zaki. Nearly shot him. And this is his man. Take him into the kitchen and give him some water. Cold water, that's the thing! On a hot day like this. Especially if you've been shot at.'

The clerk, a little hesitantly, followed behind.

'Don't worry, you're all right now. No shooting inside the house, that's the rule. She's very strict about it. No shooting inside the house! Mother!' he called. 'We have visitors. Come and meet Mr el Zaki!'

He led Mahmoud into what was obviously a reception room, the exact replica of one you would find in a rich man's house in Cairo, with a marble floor which sloped slightly down to a little indoor pool in which a fountain was playing. At one end of this room was a traditional dais, spread with leather cushions. He sat, or rather lay, on the dais and indicated that Mahmoud should lie beside him.

Then he jumped up to greet an elderly lady who had come into the room.

'This is my mother. You must meet my mother!'

She came forward. She was dressed in the conventional burka but her veil was pushed aside. She had sharp, intelligent eyes.

'This is Mr el Zaki, Mother. He has come to visit us.'

'I heard shots,' she said.

'That was me. I nearly shot Mr el Zaki.'

'It was as well that you didn't.'

'He came by the back path, you see, and I was not expecting him.'

'Even so, you should be more careful.'

'Sorry, Mother! I saw a great fat pigeon—'

'Where is the gun now? Have you put it away properly?'

'Left it at the door.'

'Unloaded?'

'Yes, Mother. Unloaded. I made sure.'

She nodded. 'Good.' Then she turned to Mahmoud. 'And what brings you here, Mr el Zaki?'

'I am from the Parquet.'

She raised her eyebrows. 'The Parquet! This is an honour. It is not often that Cairo remembers us.'

'I am investigating a case.'

'Down here? I thought the Parquet never stepped out of Cairo!'

'We do occasionally. When the case is important.'

'So this one must be.'

'Yes, it is. It concerns something sent to your husband.'

'A bomb, I hope?'

'Not quite, no. But equally shocking. A bride box.'

'Are you insane?'

'No. It was sent from Denderah. By people from this estate.'

'Now I know you are insane! A bride box? To my husband? I would have thought he'd had enough of marriage. And should it be going to him anyway? I would have thought it would be sent to her. Whoever she is.'

'The thing is, you see, the bride box was not empty.'

'Well, no, it wouldn't be.'

'It contained the body of a young girl.'

The woman's hand flew up to her throat.

'A young girl?'

'Whom I think you know,' Mahmoud added.

# FIVE

'What do you want?' asked the Pasha's lady.

'I want to talk to your servants.'

'Why?'

'Because servants from the estate brought the bride box to the railway station at Denderah and put it on the train.'

'I do not think you can be right,' said the Pasha's lady. 'It is a long way from here to Denderah on foot. Especially carrying a box.'

'Perhaps a cart?'

'You don't know what you're saying. A cart? How do you think I could spare a cart? This is a small estate. Our carts are in use.'

'It wouldn't take long to get there and back. It could be done in an afternoon.'

'And who by? Do you think I can spare servants as easily as that?'

'Nevertheless, I would like to talk to them.'

'All of them?'

'All those who work in the fields.'

'They are in the fields now.'

'Call them in. As you said, this is a small estate. It would not take long.'

The Pasha's lady laughed. 'You do not know our fellahin,' she said. 'Let them lift their heads and they won't put them down again! Not today, they won't!'

'I would not ask it if it were not important.'

'Have you tried the main house?'

'Yes.'

'And?'

'I need to try yours.'

The lady laughed again. 'Got nowhere, did you?'

'I talked to the men.'

The lady raised her eyebrows. 'Ismail let you?'

'He had them come in, and I talked to them.'

'Well, that is a surprise!'

'As I said, it is a matter of importance.'

She stood for a moment, undecided.

'I shall not keep them long,' said Mahmoud.

'It is the interruption,' said the Pasha's lady. 'The afternoon will go to pieces.'

'I would not ask it if it were not important,' he said again.

'I do not see how it could be our people,' said the lady, wavering. 'My Osman makes sure they keep their heads down. As does Ismail. That is what they are there for. Would you like to talk to Osman first?'

'It needs to be all.'

She hesitated, and then made up her mind.

'Very well,' she said. 'I will tell him to bring them in. But you must allow two hours.'

'Two hours!'

'Yes, Osman has to get there, and they are not all together. They are scattered over different fields. And then they all have to get back here.'

'Very well,' said Mahmoud, submitting to the inevitable.

The lady swept out.

'Would you like to see my guns?' asked the Pasha's son, at a loss for conversation.

'Guns?'

'I have a collection of them.'

'Well, yes, I would, please. And, may I ask, what is your name?'

'Karim. And you are Mahmoud?'

'Yes, that's right.'

'I will show you.'

He led Mahmoud along a corridor and then into a small room with racks for rifles. Dozens of them.

'These are all yours?'

'Yes. They are my collection.'

There was an old, toothless man in the room. He grinned at them and gave a half-bow.

'Ali looks after them. He oils them and that sort of thing.

You have to look after them because the sand gets in them and then it is dangerous.'

They were sporting guns, the sort of guns you would find in an English gun room. There were even some fowling pieces. Mahmoud was not an expert on guns but was impressed.

When they left, Ali locked the door.

'You can't be too careful,' said Karim. 'Not with guns.'

They went back to the *mandar'ah*, the reception room.

'Where have you been?' asked the Pasha's lady.

'I have been showing Mr el Zaki my guns, Mother.'

'Oh, yes,' she said, shrugging.

'Your son has a fine collection, my lady,' said Mahmoud.

'There is not a lot else in his life,' the Pasha's lady said.

She sat down on the dais and indicated that Mahmoud was to sit there too.

'So,' she said, 'tell me about this bride box. And this young girl.'

'She had worked here, I understand. Her name was Soraya.'

'Soraya!' said Karim.

'She did indeed work here. For a short while. Then I found her unsatisfactory and dismissed her.'

'But then you took her back?'

'Well, I was sorry for her. Perhaps I had been too hasty. And there were connections, you see, between my family and hers. Her mother came from my part of the world. Not Egypt. The Sudan. And when her mother died, I thought she would be lonely. Well, I was lonely, too. I wanted to hear my own people's speech again. Somebody told me about her and I thought, why should she not come to me and we can talk together? Her father – that awful old man – was willing. Indeed, eager. He thought he might make something out of it. And she . . . I think she was glad to get away from him. But it didn't work out. She was uncouth. I know I said there were connections between my family and hers but they were very remote connections. My family was rich, hers was poor. And her manners were . . . unsuitable. Her mother, her proper mother that is, had tried, but with that awful old man around I don't suppose she had much of a chance. Anyway, she proved unsuitable, so I sent her home.'

'But then brought her back?'

'A mistake. I shouldn't have done.'

'And then you sent her away again?'

'Yes. And I don't know what happened to her after that.'

'Did she not bring her bride box with her the second time?'

The Pasha's lady hesitated. 'Yes,' she said, 'she did. I don't know what she thought she was doing. I made her put it in one of the barns. And I suppose she took it with her when she left. And goodness knows how she happened to finish up inside.'

Karim plucked her arm. 'I don't understand, Mother. Soraya's box? And she was put inside?'

'I will explain it to you later.'

'But ought she not to be let out of the box?'

'She is no longer there. I will explain it to you.'

'But, Mother . . .'

'Go now. Go to your room.'

'But . . .'

'Now!'

Karim left the room obediently.

'He is simple,' said Karim's mother, after he had left. 'You will have seen that.'

'Yes. It is sad. I feel for you. He is a nice boy.'

'Yes,' said the Pasha's lady. 'He is.'

'And he speaks well. He speaks *English* well.'

'The words are there but not the sense. We did not realize at first. We sent him to a good school. A good *English* school. His father had hopes. "The English are masters now," he said. "Let him be brought up as an Englishman. Then he, too, will be one of the masters." But it was not to be. It soon became apparent that he was not . . . as the other boys were. At first we thought it was because he had difficulty with the different language. But then we saw that it was not. He had the words. The words came easily. But not the sense. After a while we saw that the sense was not there.

'We brought him home, here. His father did not wish anyone

to see him. He was ashamed. He blamed me. "What have you brought into the family?" he said. "There are two sides to a family," I said. "Perhaps the fault is on your side." "There has never been a monster on my side," he said. "The boy is not a monster," I said. "He is a good boy."

'"But he will never be a good man," he said. And it was true. As he grew up it became apparent that something was missing. We kept him here. His father did not want anyone to know that his son was not as other boys were. He turned his face from him, and from me also. "Take him away," he said. "Take him into another house." "If I take him, I will go with him," I said. "Go, then," he said. "For I do not wish to set eyes on him. Nor on you, either, who have brought this thing into the family." "God has brought him," I said. "And he has brought him as a punishment for your misdeeds." For I knew that my husband had not led a good life before he married me.

'Then my husband was very angry. "Did you not share in those misdeeds?" he asked. "When we sported, I did not sport alone." And it was true that we were wild when we were young. "You have brought shame into my family." "Yours is the shame," I said, "for you were a Pasha's son and I was a simple girl and I was dazzled by your magnitude. You took advantage of my innocence." "Innocence?" he scoffed. "You knew what you were doing. You had set your eyes on me and lured me into disgrace." "There was no disgrace when a son was born," I said. "When a son was born you walked proudly. It was only afterwards that you spoke of disgrace." "And disgrace it was!" he said. "To bring forth a monster!" "No," I said, "it was the hand of God, punishing us for our wrongdoing."

'He would not have it, and put me aside. But I notice that he has not married again. He fears another monster may come; and if it comes to him and not to me, then the world will know where the fault lies.' She shrugged her shoulders. 'So,' she said. 'You have heard the story. My husband wanted to hide him from the world. So I said, "You must hide me, too." And so here we both are!'

She shrugged again. Then she looked at Mahmoud. 'But

you have seen something in him?' she said. 'Something of
what he might have been?'

'Yes,' said Mahmoud.

'You are misled by the ease of the words.'

'It is not just the words,' said Mahmoud. 'Behind the words
there is something.'

She looked at him curiously. 'You think so?'

'Yes. There is kindness, there is courtesy. There is
sympathy.'

'Too much of that,' said the Pasha's lady.

'These things are not just words.'

'But words are important. Give him the words and the rest
will follow, my husband said, but at the end he was left only
with the words.'

'What was the school?' asked Mahmoud.

'The Khedivial. It was a good school. One of the best in
Cairo. There was nothing wrong with the school. But it wasn't
right for him.'

'I know the school. It is a little too military in style
for me.'

'That was the attraction for my husband,' said the Pasha's
lady. 'He thought it would strengthen Karim. He thought that
was what he needed. Discipline. He thought he just wasn't
trying. Of course, it wasn't that. No amount of discipline,
drilling, saluting and that sort of thing could help poor Karim.
When I saw that I took him away. My husband was angry.
But why should I let the poor boy be shouted at when it was
obviously not his fault?'

'You did the right thing,' said Mahmoud.

She looked at him, surprised, then amazed. 'You think so,
do you?'

'If he was struggling.'

'Well, he was struggling. He needed help, not shouting.'

'Did you try to give him help?'

'I gave him lessons myself.' She shrugged. 'But that was
not much good. I am not learned, as his father is. I did not
know what was required. So I brought in a tutor. A well-
meaning fool, who couldn't seem to grasp that Karim was . . .
different. I told him to go, and after that Karim was left to

himself. He was happier like that. Sometimes though, I can
see he is bored.'

'There are places which can help.'

'What sort of places?'

'Schools. Special schools.'

'At his age?' She shook her head. 'No, he would feel out
of place.'

'There are teachers with special skills. Trained to help people
like Karim.'

'In Egypt?'

'Perhaps not in Egypt,' conceded Mahmoud. 'Not in Egypt
*yet*,' he said.

She laughed. 'Ah, you're not one of those! You believe
in improving things, do you? Reforms? Don't let my
husband hear that!' She leaned forward and touched him
on the knee.

'You're very young,' she said.

'Perhaps,' said Mahmoud. 'But these things happen. In
Europe there are special skills for people such as Karim. Even
as old as he is.'

'But that's Europe.'

'We too can be like that,' said Mahmoud.

She looked at him curiously. 'Well,' she said, 'you *are* an
odd one! Parquet officers must be different these days!'

'Things are changing. People are changing.'

'They won't change fast enough,' said the Pasha's lady. 'Not
for people like Karim.'

At least there had been no difficulty this time. Within the hour
men were beginning to assemble in the yard. There would be
fewer of them. The lady's estate was smaller than the other
one. He went out into the yard and watched them arrive. He
took the clerk out with him and told him to sit down with his
back against the wall. And to cover his face.

The clerk needed no reminding. He unwrapped his turban
and then wrapped some of the folds about his face. One or
two of the men looked at him curiously but mostly they hardly
even noticed that he was there.

Some of the women servants came out from the house, as

before at the other house, and stood there watching. There
were not many exciting things to see on an estate in Upper
Egypt.

Osman came up to him. 'They are all here, Effendi.'

Mahmoud spoke to them as before. They listened uninter-
estedly, their faces blank. A train? A station? Denderah? None
of it registered. 'Do they ever go to Denderah?' he whispered
to Osman.

'Not often, Effendi.'

They stayed on the estate and worked. Which, of course,
suited the Pasha and his lady. That was how things seemed
to be in Upper Egypt. The fellahin were bound to the estate,
as their fathers had been. They knew nothing other than work.
How were they to be raised to take an interest in things?
thought Mahmoud. It ate into them, this monotonous labour
in the fields. It reduced them. In Cairo life was vibrant. There
was always talk, chatter. Did the men here ever talk when
they were in the fields? Perhaps not. It was too hot, the work
too draining. In the evenings after the day's work was done
perhaps then they could talk. But even then, he thought, after
the work in the fields, they had probably been too emptied
of energy.

In a desperate attempt to get a flicker of interest, he moved
on to the bride box. Even then, though, he got nowhere.

He told them to sit down. Then, apparently casually, he
began to stroll around. In doing so he passed close to the clerk
sitting, face muffled, against the wall.

'Well?' he whispered.

The muffled figure shook his head.

'These are not the men, Effendi,' the clerk said.

So he had been barking up the wrong tree. The clerk had
been mistaken and sent him on a wild goose chase. Or maybe,
and this was not unlikely, the men who had brought the box
had lied to him. They were not from the estate, neither of the
estates. They came from somewhere else.

And yet they had mentioned the Pasha specifically by
name. And they had definitely meant the box to go to him.

Obviously, there was someone in the area who had a

grudge against him. It meant more casting around, he thought glumly, more time spent in this hell hole; while all the time Aisha and the children were having to get along without him.

How long was he going to be here? Forever? He must be right. Someone had it in for him. He must have crossed someone back in Cairo.

And he could do nothing about it! He had been stitched up nice and truly. That's it, Mahmoud, goodbye to your career!

He dismissed the men and for the first time they showed signs of life, even venturing a monosyllable or two of conversation as they left.

The women servants turned away. Not much to see then! Disappointing.

Nevertheless, he went over to them. 'You knew Soraya,' he said.

'We knew Soraya,' they said warily.

'And saw her bride box?'

There was division here: some had seen the bride box, others not.

'It was taken away,' someone explained. 'And put in the barn. And then we did not see it any more.'

'Did she show it to you?'

They shook their heads.

'Once,' one of them qualified.

'You went out to the barn?'

'She showed it to me when it was still in the house.'

'Just after she had come back?'

'That is so.'

'And did you think she had nice things?'

'Quite nice,' someone said.

'Nice, but showy. I have nicer things.'

'You have a bride box yourself?'

The woman nodded.

'And when are you to be married?'

'Not yet.'

'Just waiting,' explained another woman.

'For someone to ask for her?'

'For Abdul to make up his mind!'

There was a general laugh.

'And was Soraya, too, just waiting?'

'It would seem so,' some said.

'Do you think she was wrong to bring her bride box here?'

On the whole they thought it was.

'It was too presumptuous,' someone said.

'Her man had not yet spoken for her?'

He didn't get a reply.

'Perhaps he had not made up his mind?' said Mahmoud with a smile.

Again there was silence.

'You women are all in trouble,' said Mahmoud, smiling, 'if your men are not going to speak!'

'It wasn't that.'

'Ah? What was it?'

But again there was silence.

'The lady would not have it.'

'Perhaps the lady did not want to lose her,' said Mahmoud. 'Having only just brought her back?'

Again there was the silence.

'She seemed to hold her dear,' said Mahmoud.

'She did, at first.'

'It was "Soraya do this, Soraya do that! Soraya come and sit near me, Soraya come and talk to me!"'

'I expect she wanted to hear her own tongue?' said Mahmoud.

'Well, yes, but she could always have gone and visited her family if she had missed her own people so much!'

'*Does* she miss them?' asked Mahmoud.

'I think she does. She is always sending them gifts.'

'It was like that with the Pasha, too. He was always sending them gifts.'

'At first.'

'Well, he kept on with it. Even after . . .' the woman stopped.

'After the Pasha had put her aside?'

'After she had come to live here with the young Pasha – even then he continued to send them gifts. Still does, they say. I wonder why? It's not even that her people are . . . well, our people. They are all Sudanis. Gifts, messages, and I don't know what else! They turn up at the house, and Ismail receives them graciously, which is more than he does with other people. He has to, or the Pasha will fall on him, he says.'

'So what does he do with them when the Pasha is not at home?'

'Sends them on to Cairo. Ismail even has to find the money. He doesn't like it, of course, but he has to do what the Pasha has ordered, and no nonsense about it! But why the Pasha makes such a fuss over them, I cannot think. Particularly as he won't have anything to do with his wife or son. It's a strange old world!'

'And she's no better. Always sending messages. Suleiman is away now.'

'No, he's not. I saw him here this morning.'

'Yes, he is. I saw him go. Late this morning. In a hurry.'

'Well, I wonder what that's about? Mind you, you never know. She won't say and he won't say.'

'Who is Suleiman?' asked Mahmoud.

'My lady's man.'

'He works in the fields?'

'No, no, he's too grand for that. About the house. He's another Sudani. Comes from the lady's family. Always going back there to do this or that.'

'Sudani?' said Mahmoud. 'Like Soraya?'

'Closer. Soraya's not really part of her family. Well, she is, but not really. A distant cousin. Very distant, I know, because I heard them talking once, she and the lady. They were trying to puzzle out the family connection. And not finding it easy, I must say. But it did exist. The lady remembers Soraya's mother.'

'And Suleiman went off?' said Mahmoud. 'This morning?'

'Yes. In a hurry, like I said.'

'That would be before the men came in from the fields?'

'Just before. He was leaving as they were arriving.'

'But . . .' began Mahmoud.

The Pasha's lady had known that the servants would be

parading before him, had agreed to it herself. And then she had done this! Made sure he wouldn't speak to everybody. Not, almost certainly, to the one person with whom he wanted to speak.

They had done it again. Tricked him.

But this time there was a difference. He now knew exactly who the Pasha's lady did not want him to speak to.

One day Zeinab came back home to hear shrieks inside the house. She dropped the packages she was holding and rushed in. Leila was standing in the kitchen sobbing. She held her arms out and Zeinab, without thinking, grabbed her and held her close.

Neither Musa nor his wife were to be seen. They had gone out to the market, Leila explained between sobs. They were buying a lot of things and Musa, unusually among Egyptian men, had gone to help carry them. And she, Leila, had tripped over the step and blooded her knee!

She showed Zeinab the knee fearfully.

It was indeed bloody but not a mortal wound, and Zeinab, who, in her father's house would normally have shouted for a slave, reckoned she could cope on her own. She carried Leila, still racked with sobs, into the bathroom and sponged the blood off.

'Look!' she said. 'It's all gone!'

Leila peered doubtfully; then saw a part where the skin had come off and opened her mouth to roar again.

'We'll put a patch on it,' said Zeinab hastily. There were, she knew, patches in the cupboard. Owen sometimes used one when he cut himself shaving. She found one and spread it over the wounded area.

Leila, curious, cut off her scream in mid-roar.

'It will be all right now,' said Zeinab reassuringly.

Still the little body heaved and Zeinab hugged her tight. Eventually the sobbing subsided, but Zeinab went on holding her. She found she quite liked the experience. It came to her that not all things should be delegated to slaves.

Musa and his wife returned at this point. Musa's wife rushed across and took over from Zeinab. And Musa patted his heart and said he had heard the shouts and feared Leila was dying.

'Would you mind?' asked Leila.

'A bit,' said Musa.

Leila knew he was teasing her. She broke into chuckles and soon the incident was forgotten.

But not by Zeinab. She had seen the way that Musa's wife handled Leila, and she had observed the way her friend Aisha behaved with her children, and she guessed that this was the way mothers behaved with their children. When she came back into the kitchen, after collecting the purchases she had dropped, she gave Leila a hug.

Leila put her arm round her neck and gave her a kiss. Then she climbed up on to Zeinab's lap. 'You have a lovely smell, Auntie,' she said.

'Thank you!' said Zeinab. 'It's perfume.'

'It's in your ear,' said Leila.

'Not *in* my ear but behind it,' said Zeinab. 'Would you like to try some?'

After this they were more at ease with each other. Zeinab even took her with her sometimes when she went shopping in the fashionable, almost entirely French, great stores.

One day when they were out together, Leila tugged at her arm and said: 'Auntie, why is that man looking at me?'

'Which man?'

'He has gone away now.'

'Are you sure he was looking at you?'

'Oh, yes.'

'I expect he was thinking what a pretty little girl you are.'

'I don't think he was thinking that,' said Leila doubtfully.

Zeinab let it pass but she remembered Owen's worries that the slavers might try to steal Leila back and decided to keep her eyes open in future. Once or twice she saw a man look at Leila in a way that troubled her but in each case Leila said it was not the man who had looked at her before. Zeinab mentioned it to Musa's wife and she said she would talk to Musa about it so that he could be on his guard, too.

Zeinab also told her friend Aisha about it, but Aisha said that men were always looking at young girls in a troubling way and she doubted if there was any real matter for concern. However, Zeinab thought she would mention it to Owen when he got back, which she hoped would be soon.

# SIX

There was an unfamiliar face at the station, belonging to the man standing in for the clerk. He said that he was the clerk's brother and that he had done the job before. He was familiar with the duties. His name, he said, was Babikr.

Owen asked him about the station. How much traffic was there? Lots, said Babikr. But, on further enquiry, it didn't seem to amount to that much, merely the train coming up from Luxor once a day and then a corresponding train returning south late in the afternoon. Sometimes a goods train passed through, usually at night. It must have been this train that Leila had seen and then hidden under. Trains stopped at Denderah for water and to drop or pick up packages. Like the bride box, thought Owen. There wasn't a lot of business of this sort.

Owen asked if he knew of a white man who had come to Denderah recently on business.

Babikr nodded.

'That would be Clarke Effendi,' he said. 'He trades in gum arabic and trocchee shells. The desert men' – this was said with a certain contempt – 'bring the gum in on their camels. It gets divided here and sent to different destinations, some on the coast, some in the big cities. A lot goes to Cairo. Clarke Effendi comes to see to that himself. He does not keep a man in Denderah.'

Babikr said that Clarke Effendi did not come often. He would wait, perhaps for months, for the stocks of gum arabic to build up and then would come with a big caravan to take it away. He combined this with a large trade in trocchee shells. On the outward journey from the coast to Denderah he would bring trocchee shells, which again would be distributed from Denderah. Most would go up to Cairo, from where they would be distributed to factories inland, but some would go straight to Alexandria or Port Said for export abroad. The shells went all over the world, some as far as America.

Having deposited trocchee shells in Denderah, the caravan would pick up gum arabic for the return journey. It was a big operation, said Babikr, and it all came together at Denderah. For over a week Denderah would be transformed.

'You wouldn't recognize it, Effendi.'

The space behind the station, about the size of two football fields, would be given over to camels and their drivers. The incoming loads of trocchee shells and gum arabic would be divided and subdivided and re-consigned. All, said Babikr, was bustle and busyness.

And over it all, Clarke Effendi presided in person. He had assistants, of course, mostly Levantines from the north, but he watched over it all like a hawk. 'Trusting no one,' said Babikr in admiration.

Miraculously, in little more than a week, it would all get sorted out. The trocchee shells would go one way, the gum arabic another. The desert men would go back to their gum trees, the caravan, its camels now loaded up with bales of gum arabic, back to the coast. The space behind the station would become empty and all, said Babikr, would be still again.

But the Effendi would see for himself if he stayed on. For the caravan was due to arrive the following week.

'Ah!' said Owen. 'And Clarke Effendi with it?'

'Most certainly! For he likes to keep an eye on all things.'

'And does he sometimes come to Denderah on other occasions?'

'As the time for the great caravan nears, he will come over on several occasions, to make sure that the suppliers of gum arabic are coming in as expected.'

'Has he been recently?'

'Oh, yes. And then he had been angry because he had thought that not enough had come in, and he had sent men to chide the suppliers. With some result, for the bales are now coming in thick and fast. Effendi, you will no doubt have seen how they are piling up at the station.'

'And does the caravan sometimes bring things besides trocchee shells?'

'Oh, yes, Effendi! This is the main caravan of the year,
now that the huge pilgrim caravans of the past are dwindling
in importance with the coming of the trains. Many ordinary
people wish to send things from east to west, or from west
to east, and not trusting the new postal system, will make use
of it.'

'What sort of things?'

'Things for the bazaars, Effendi. Or presents to the
family.'

'Bride boxes?' suggested Owen.

'Oh, no! Effendi!' said Babikr, shocked. And knowing
perfectly well what Owen was thinking.

Owen found Mustapha sitting in his small yard, his work
things spread out on the ground around him. A half-finished
basket was held between his knees. Some reeds ready for
threading were stuck between his toes. He looked up listlessly
as Owen came into the yard.

'Effendi!'

'Mustapha,' said Owen, squatting down beside him, 'I need
you to tell me more.'

'I have told you all, Effendi,' said the basket maker.

'Not quite all. Tell me about the slaver.'

Mustapha shrugged. 'What is there to tell? He was a slaver.
That is all.'

'How did you come upon him?'

'People said that he was in the neighbourhood.'

'He was a Sudani. Did you go to him because he was a
Sudani?'

'Why should I go to him because he was a Sudani?'

'Was not your wife a Sudani?'

'I did not go to him because of that.'

'No?'

'I thought it might help,' said Mustapha, after a moment.

'Tell me about her. How came it that you met her? The
Sudan is far from here.'

'She came back with the Pasha when he brought his

new wife. She brought servants and Hoseina was one of them.
After a time she sought a husband. I had a friend who knew
someone in the Pasha's household and he spoke for me. I
was doing well then. I promised to be a man of substance.'

'How comes it that you did not become a man of
substance?'

'Children,' said Mustapha bitterly.

'You had too many?'

'I could not provide for them. And they came too quickly
for Hoseina. She ailed and could not manage the house.
But still they came. It broke her down. And I could not
provide.'

'Did you not speak to the Pasha's lady and ask for help?'

'I did, and at first she helped us. But then she had troubles
of her own and forgot about us.'

'I wondered if perhaps the reason she took Soraya on to
help in her house was that she remembered your wife?'

'In part, yes. But it did not work out. She came home again
and I thought that was the end of it. So when the slaver came
. . . when the slaver came and said there was a man who had
his eye on Soraya, my heart rejoiced. He said he would arrange
it all. He did not speak of her as a slave, Effendi, but as . . .
more than that.'

'A concubine?'

'Well, perhaps to start with. But it might grow, Effendi.
These things have happened, I have known of them
happening. And I thought it might be so with Soraya. She
was not ill-favoured. The slaver himself said that. He said
that affection might grow in the man's heart, and then, who
knew? He said the man had already noticed her, the seeds
were already there. He spoke of it as a likely thing. More
than likely; almost a certain thing. And I . . . I believed
him, Effendi. I was a fool, yes I know, but I did not wish
her harm, Effendi. She was my daughter, after all. But there
were difficulties in the house, and besides, money was
promised . . .'

'Was money given?'

'A little, Effendi, a little. But more was promised. And,
besides, Effendi . . .'

'Yes?'

'The slaver spoke of it as a done thing. I thought of it as a done thing. And so I asked him if I should send the bride box with her, and when he laughed and said, "Why not?" I believed it to be certain.'

He shook his head.

'I still cannot believe it, Effendi. Why should he kill her? As he himself said, she was a beautiful girl who would surely fetch a good bride price. So why kill her, Effendi? That is what I cannot understand.'

'Tell me more about the slaver, Abdulla Sardawi. Where does he come from?'

'Suakin.'

'Suakin? The Dead City? Is that likely?'

'Not many live there, Effendi, but he does.'

'So that he may more easily slip his slaves across the sea?'

'So they say, Effendi.'

'I hope you are telling me truly. If so it may go some way towards reducing the punishment that awaits you. But if not, expect the punishment to be heavier.'

'I have told you truly, Effendi. I tell you not because of the punishment. Let it fall upon me; I have deserved it. I tell it for Soraya. I tell it for the daughter who was once mine.'

Owen went back to the railway station. Mahmoud and the clerk were not yet back and the clerk's brother was still standing as substitute.

'Babikr . . .'

'Effendi?'

'Can you send a cable?'

'I can, Effendi. I am a master of all the arts.'

'Good. Well, send this one, then. It is to the Sudan.'

'There will be no difficulty, Effendi. It will go straight to Khartoum.'

'I wish it to go to the Slavery Bureau.'

The clerk's brother handed him a pad. 'Write your message there, Effendi, and I will send it at once. Within the moment.'

Owen took the pad and wrote:

*Request assistance. Slaver active in Upper Egypt area.*
*Believed based in Suakin. Possibly returning there with*
*child slaves. Name Sardawi, Abdulla Sardawi.*
*The Mamur Zapt.*

A long line of camels had just come in and were unloading
their bales beside the rail tracks. The stacks of gum arabic
had suddenly grown, and in the town itself there were more
people. Many of them were from the desert and they wandered
around the shops, not buying but looking at the wares. The
space behind the station was filling up. After depositing their
loads the camels had moved on to the square and were tearing
at the forage thrown down on the ground for them to eat.
Beside them sat their drivers, sometimes around a brazier,
drinking tea. They were a different kind of Arab from the
ones seen in the town, thin, wiry, with short galabeyas showing
knees burned almost black by the sun. Some of them had
great masses of fuzzy hair. These were Kipling's 'Fuzzy-
Wuzzies' and they came from the other side of the Sudan,
near the coast, from the Red Sea Hills. They often had short
stabbing spears. One or two merchants were already setting
up stalls in anticipation of the caravan's arrival.

Seeing the shoppers reminded Owen that he would be
returning to Cairo the next day – he had already spent far
too long away from his desk – and he ought to take something back for Zeinab. And also for Leila. He mustn't forget
about her!

But what? He had never bought for a child before and had
no idea of what to buy. A toy of some kind? But they didn't
seem to have toys in the shops here. In Cairo it would have
been no problem, but here . . .

Clothes? He would do a lot better in Cairo, where he would
be able to draw on other people's expertise. Zeinab, perhaps,
was not the world's expert on anything for children, but
Georgiades's Rosa was sure to have a sharp eye for these
things. Nikos, of course, would be a dead loss.

And then there was the question of size. He knew roughly
what size Leila was but not in the way a woman would. Better
steer clear of clothes.

Slippers, say. There were some nice little embroidered ones in the shops here. She would like those. But again there was the question of size. He had an uneasy feeling that the ones here would be too small for Leila. He rather thought her feet were quite big in relation to her general size. Maybe feet grew first? Again he was venturing into areas new to him. If the slippers wouldn't fit, they would be useless. Better steer clear of footwear.

But what then? Material? One or two of the shops had what seemed to him quite attractive lengths of material. But he could hear Zeinab dismissing them scathingly over his shoulder. They might do for Musa's wife, he thought, but for Leila?

He was going to buy a carved wooden bracelet for Zeinab, something made locally and with a curiosity value. Would that do for Leila as well?

He was passing a carpenter's shop. It was just an empty space with a few planks leaning against the walls. There was no counter. In the other shops, as in the less sophisticated parts of Cairo, there would have been a counter, with a shopkeeper sitting on it. There was one like that nearby, the one where they sold materials. But the carpenter's shop was not like that.

He could see the carpenter working away in the back of the shop. He looked up and came across to Owen. 'Does the Effendi desire anything?'

'Advice,' said Owen. He explained the situation.

'What I would give my grandchildren,' said the carpenter, 'is something I had made. A spoon, perhaps? Like this.'

He produced some long, finely carved spoons.

'That looks pretty good!' said Owen, relieved.

'Or this. To keep things in. Children always like something like this.' He produced a little box.

Why not? It was small, about six inches long, made of nice wood. Sandalwood? It was smooth, pleasant to touch and agreeably smelling.

'I'll take it.'

'Wait! Wait! Some paper, Selim. Go to Ali's and ask him for some nice paper to wrap a present in, a present for a little girl.'

A boy at the back of the shop rushed out. There seemed something familiar about him. Selim?

'Is that the Selim who came with me to the old temple? And found the things from Soraya's bride box?'

'Yes, it is. I don't like to think of that, Effendi. Soraya was a sweet girl. I made her bride box for her. To think of the use it was put to! Oh, Effendi, there are wicked men in the world!'

He shook his head.

'But you're right, Effendi, it was Selim who found the things.' He looked around furtively, but Selim was not yet back. 'Between you and me, Effendi, there was something between Selim and Soraya. He has not been the same boy since. I try to keep him busy but you can tell his heart's not in it.'

The boy returned and began to wrap up the box.

'This is for Leila,' said Owen quietly. 'I will tell her that you wrapped the box.'

Mahmoud was getting ready to leave. By the time he and the clerk got back to Denderah it would have long been dark, but there was no point in staying here. He had done what he could. He had hoped that, with the clerk's aid, he would have been able to wrap the whole thing up. They would have identified the men who had put Soraya in the bride box. They would probably be the men who had killed her but even if they weren't, it could have opened the whole thing up. The end would have been in sight and so would have been his return to Cairo. Cairo, and his family. Mahmoud was missing his children. He had never been away from them for so long before.

But it hadn't worked out like that. There had been no identifications. He was no further on than when he had started. Although perhaps he was. Not as far on as he had hoped, but at least he had been given a lead.

He called the clerk to him and told him to let it be known that Mahmoud would like to know when Suleiman returned. And there would be money in it. The clerk was to drop this in casually. Mahmoud had not been able to speak to Suleiman while he was here. As they knew, Suleiman had gone off on an errand for the lady, so Mahmoud had missed him. But he still wanted to talk to everyone, to make sure that he had spoken to all the lady's servants. All, without exception. He wanted to be sure that he hadn't missed anything. And so he would be grateful if he could be told when Suleiman had got back. And, as the clerk had said, there would be money in it.

More than that he could not do. At least for the moment. It wasn't much but it was something. He might still be able to extract something from his visit to the Pasha's estate. To both the houses. That at least he had learned.

At the last moment, as he was setting out for Denderah, the lady appeared. Give it another hour, she said. It would be cooler then. The sun's heat would have gone from the ground, and it would be much nicer for travelling. True, it would be dark, but she would send someone with him to show him the way. Mahmoud accepted the offer gratefully. He could still feel the day's heat in the air, and both he and certainly the clerk had just about had enough of it.

A servant brought him lemonade in the mandar'ah. Karim looked in once or twice, friendly but at a loss for conversation. He offered to show Mahmoud his guns, having apparently forgotten that he had already done so. Mahmoud politely declined.

The lady herself did not appear.

A servant came and said that Salah was now waiting. Mahmoud went out into the yard, where the donkeys were standing docilely. Salah was a short, stocky man who presumably worked in the lady's fields. At the last moment Karim came out to say farewell. He said he would walk with them a little of the way.

As they went past the barns Mahmoud saw that activity of some sort was going on. The doors, which he had previously seen locked, were now open and men were bringing out heavy boxes. In the torch light something glistened.

'It's the guns,' said Karim.

'From your collection?'

'No, no; these are the ones we've been storing for Hafiz.'

Mahmoud could count six boxes. There might be more inside the barn. 'That's a lot of guns,' he said.

'Yes,' said Karim casually.

They moved on past.

'Yakub will be sending someone to collect them tomorrow,' said Karim. 'Sometimes he brings a gun for me.'

'Really?'

'Yes, a present. Mother says it's a way of saying thank you. I hope he gives me one of these. They're a new model. It's the sights, mostly – they've improved them. And certainly that would be a help with the small birds.'

They came to the edge of the out buildings.

'Well, I must turn back,' said Karim. He held out his hand. 'Nice to have met you, Mr el Zaki.'

'A pleasure to meet both you and your mother,' returned Mahmoud. 'Give her my thanks for her hospitality, will you?'

'I will,' promised Karim.

The night was soft and warm. Once they had got away from the house it seemed pitch dark but gradually their eyes grew accustomed to the darkness and the track ahead was easily visible. It threaded its way through the thorn bushes. The donkeys padded softly along.

Mahmoud drew alongside Salah. 'What is all this about the guns?' he asked.

'The Pasha's lady keeps them in her barn until the great caravan comes,' he said. 'Then they send someone over to pick them up.'

'And take them on to Denderah?'

'That is right, yes.'

'They don't come with the caravan?'

'They came with a smaller caravan earlier,' said Salah. 'Then they are left here.'

'Who brings them?'

'Yakub.'

'In another caravan?'

'In another caravan, yes. Yakub has camels of his own, which he hires out.'

'Someone hires him to bring the guns?'

'That's right, yes.'

He didn't seem disposed to say more. Perhaps he didn't know more.

Gradually it became lighter, and Mahmoud realized that the moon had risen. It shone a silvery light on everything. It was almost as bright as day.

The night now was still warm but the heat was gentle. Mahmoud realized that the lady had been right. It was a much better time to travel.

Mahmoud was thinking about the guns. Although they were not particularly his concern on this occasion, they were of concern to anyone responsible for law and order in Egypt. Owen, he knew, would be interested. The governor kept a close watch on the illicit movement of guns. And this 'movement' was surely illicit. He would remember the names and pass them on to Owen. Yakub – it might come in useful.

The soft padding of the donkey's feet and the slow, regular movement was quite soporific. He felt himself nodding off, and jerked himself awake.

The clerk, he saw, had bent so far forward over the donkey's neck that he looked in danger of falling off. He was almost certainly asleep. Mahmoud wondered whether to wake him but decided not to. It would pass the night more quickly for him and, on the whole, it looked as if he was not going to actually fall.

Just as Mahmoud thought that, the clerk *did* fall, but forward over the donkey's neck. He gave a start and raised himself. When Mahmoud looked again he was inclining forward once more.

Mahmoud himself must have dozed off because when he next took stock of his surroundings, the moonlight had become a drabber grey. He fancied he could see touches of dawn in the sky. He suddenly realized that he was very stiff and more than a little sore. This was the longest ride he had had on a donkey for many years, if ever. And he hoped it would be as long again before he had another one!

The next time he looked up he saw palm trees and

buildings. He made out the black water tank of the railway station. Camels. People. Far more camels and people than when he had left, surely?

Owen found the omda hoeing a piece of land at the end of the town. He looked up when he saw Owen and wiped his forehead.

'Effendi!' he said, pleased to stop.

'A question,' said Owen, 'about Soraya's bride box. It was, we all agree, sent after her. But where to? It is said that it was sent to the Pasha's lady's house, and that she was angered when she saw it arriving. But I have just been speaking with Mustapha, and Mustapha says that it was the slaver who came for Soraya. And that when Mustapha asked him if he should send the bride box with her, the slaver laughed and said: "Why not?" The slaver said he knew of someone who had his eye on Soraya, and Mustapha understood that Soraya was going to him. And so he sent the bride box. But what happened then? Because the next thing we hear is that Soraya is again with the Pasha's lady. And so is her bride box. Does this man exist? And if not, why should the slaver say he did? And how comes it that then Soraya and the bride box go to the Pasha's lady's house?'

The omda scratched his head. 'I know not,' he said.

'The men who came for Soraya's box – were they the slaver's men? Or the Pasha's lady's men?'

'The slaver's men, surely.'

'And yet the box turned up in the lady's house. Did Soraya know that it was going to the lady's house, or did she think it was going to a man the slaver knew of?'

'I do not think she thought she was going back to the lady's house. She thought, and Mustapha thought, that she was going to a man the slaver was acting for. "Leave it to me," he said, "and I will arrange all." We all thought that she was going to her marriage. The slaver spoke so. And she herself believed it, so when Mustapha spoke to her about it, she said she would not go to him unless she thought him worthy. And Mustapha was angered and wanted to beat her, but we restrained him.'

'And yet she finished up at the Pasha's lady's house?'

'It seems so.'

'I find that hard to understand.'

'It must be a trick. Men such as the slaver are full of tricks.'

Mahmoud had ridden into Denderah just before dawn. He had discharged the lady's guide, the station clerk, and the donkeys and then snatched some sleep for himself. Only a little, for there were things to do. But he was good at waking himself up and midway through the morning he went to find Owen. He met him just coming back from talking to the omda. They walked back together to the station, where the stacks of gum arabic were growing all the time, and then out behind the station to what had been, when Mahmoud left, a vast, empty square but which was now brimming with people and camels and donkeys. Some stalls had been set up selling tea and Owen and Mahmoud ordered some from one of them. The man brought it to them sitting on the ground.

They had information to exchange. Owen needed to know about the guns and Mahmoud brought him up to date with the failure to identify any of the Pasha's men – but also the possible lead with Suleiman. Owen shared with him the conflicting information about the destination of Soraya's bride box.

In both cases the exchange brought about a switch in thinking. Mahmoud realized that he would have to go back to the Pasha's estate and the lady's house; Owen, who had been intending to return to Cairo, thought that in the light of what Mahmoud had told him about the guns – and what he had learned at the temple – he would stay on in Denderah for another couple of days, at least until the caravan had arrived bringing its miscellaneous cargoes.

As they were drinking the tea, Owen heard himself hailed. It was the clerk's brother, Babikr, and he was moving a slip of paper.

'For you, Effendi! For you!'

It was a reply to his cable to the Sudan Slavery Bureau. It read:

*Abdulla Sardawi known to us. Bugger! Thought he'd retired.*
*Will keep an eye and nab on return to Suakin.*
*Macfarlane.*

Afterwards, Mahmoud wandered off around the square and
Owen went back to the railway station. A train had just come
in but it was the passenger train from Luxor, not a goods train
and had no effect on the great wall of gum arabic sacks that
had sprung up.

Not many people got off the passenger train. This was not
yet the tourist season and there were few visitors for Denderah:
one or two Levantines in suits, merchants, perhaps, taking
advantage of the great cross-over of goods, and a family
returning to Denderah to be met by a great gang of relatives.
Come for a wedding, perhaps? Or a funeral?

But there was also a tall, thin man in a white suit, a
European of sorts. He wore a straw hat, pulled forward over
his face against the sun, and dark sunglasses that he kept
pulling off to see better. What he seemed to be looking at
were the sacks of gum arabic, which he scrutinized very
closely.

Some time later Owen had the feeling that he was being
watched. This was something about which you developed a
sixth sense if you were a Cairo policeman, and Owen, almost
as a matter of habit, moved away into the shadows where he
was less obvious.

Then he looked around himself. At first he couldn't spot
who had been watching him, but he was sure someone had
been. And then he caught sight of him: it was the tall, thin
European who had got off the train.

To the best of his knowledge Owen had never seen the
man before, so why he should be watching him, he couldn't
think.

The man moved away and Owen almost forgot about him.
But not quite.

Sometime later he felt the man's gaze on him again. He was
standing by some camels and he slipped behind him and looked
back. It was the man again, the same man. And he was

definitely watching Owen. When Owen passed behind the camels the man began to search around for him.

Owen showed himself and walked off. A little later, he looked back – and, yes, there was the man again.

Who was he? What was he doing? And why should he be watching Owen?

He didn't look, from his clothes, as if he was from Denderah. The train had come from Luxor, but this man looked as if he had come straight from Cairo.

And that put another complexion on it. There were plenty of people in Cairo with something against the Mamur Zapt. But why come down to Denderah to attack him? In Cairo it could be done more easily and less obtrusively. And who was it, anyway? Owen began to run through the list – the rather long list – of those who might have a score to settle.

Owen began to stalk the stalker. It wasn't easy to do it without being observed. There weren't that many Europeans in the crowd thronging the square. But one of the few was the man he was trying to keep an eye on, and he stood out as much as Owen himself did.

At first the man seemed nonplussed when he lost sight of Owen, but after hovering about uncertainly for a moment or two he seemed to shrug and move away. Owen followed him as he went through the bales of gum arabic. He seemed to be checking numbers as much as their condition. But then a train of camels moved between them and he lost sight of the man.

It left Owen with a feeling of discomfort and puzzlement. He hadn't expected this, not out of Cairo.

# SEVEN

Owen had called Nikos, the official clerk, and told him to find out what he could about the trader, Clarke, and one day a fat, slovenly dressed Greek came up to the warehouse from which Clarke operated when he was in Cairo.

He wasn't in Cairo very often, the clerk in the warehouse explained to the Greek when he inquired. In fact, he had just missed him. He travelled a great deal, mostly in Upper Egypt, visiting suppliers of gum arabic and seeing how the trees they harvested were doing that year. He liked to see the stocks before buying them, and then he often accompanied the caravan to Denderah from where they were distributed throughout the Sudan and Egypt and often, these days, abroad. He always took particular care when the gum was going abroad as he wanted to be sure that it was not adulterated on the way. Quality, Clarke had emphasized, was important in foreign markets. And the Sudanis – and indeed anyone who lived in Upper Egypt – were not wholly to be trusted. Clarke Effendi was always having trouble with someone or other. He had often said to Fuad, the clerk in the warehouse, that unless you stood right over them, they were always up to something. So Clarke Effendi was often away standing right over them.

The Greek said that things were not that different in Cairo. The clerk agreed and said that he personally had to keep a sharp eye on the men who worked in the warehouse. Clarke Effendi had enjoined him to keep a particular eye on stock loss through pilfering.

'Of gum arabic?' said the Greek, surprised. 'Wouldn't that be hard to steal?'

'No, no, not gum. That is in great slabs and would not be worth the effort. But Clarke Effendi also trades in other things and they are more stealable. Trinkets for the bazaars. Jewellery for the unwary. And, of course, trocchee shells.'

'Trocchee shells?'

'Oh, yes.' It was big business. Shells from Egypt and the Sudan went all over the world. He, the Greek, would be surprised at the places the shells went to: Europe, Italy, especially, America – New York was the place – and even India and China. Clarke Effendi was always saying that he ought to pay a visit to the Far East. A visit, he claimed, would certainly double sales there. But so far he had not gone.

They went round the corner to continue their chat over a cup of coffee. The Greek was good at chatting. His big, brown, sympathetic eyes invited confidences. That was why Owen employed him. Georgiades was his name.

He gave confidences in return. Mostly about his wife, whom he loved dearly but who terrified him. She was a business woman. Well, yes, that was unusual, but she was an unusual woman. A whiz at figures. That sort of thing always made Georgiades himself uneasy. She played the Cairo Bourse, the Egyptian Stock Exchange. When Georgiades had first found out, he had been paralysed with fear and demanded that she stay at home like a decent woman and look after the children.

'On your money?' she had said. 'We couldn't even afford to buy them shoes!'

This, unfortunately, was true, and he had agreed to let her continue. But only for a short while and with the tiniest of sums. And never, never, never was there to be any risk.

'Sure, sure, sure!' said Rosa, but the Greek was not entirely convinced that she followed his instruction. ('Women are like that,' said Fuad.)

Anyway, the children always seemed to be well off for shoes, so Georgiades thought it best not to enquire too closely. And then there was the question of the house.

'House?'

They had just, at Rosa's insistence, moved into a yet bigger one. Georgiades had torn his hair.

'But the cost!' he had wailed. 'How do I find the money?'

'I'll find the money,' said Rosa.

'But how?'

'I'll double the trade.'

Georgiades didn't know what this meant but he didn't like the sound of it.

'Is there not risk?' he had asked timidly.

'Oh, yes,' said Rosa. 'But I'll cover that with a reverse trade.'

Georgiades didn't like the sound of this, either. In fact, it terrified him.

And the warehouse clerk, too. 'May Allah preserve you!' he gasped.

Georgiades hoped he would but rather doubted it. 'I shall end up in prison!' he had wailed.

'You will, but I won't,' said Rosa cheerfully. 'It's all in your name, so I'll still be able to look after the children.'

'The wickedness of women!' cried the warehouse clerk, his sympathies totally engaged.

'The trouble is,' said Georgiades, 'she takes on riskier and riskier things! Arms, for instance . . .'

'Ah, well,' said the warehouse clerk, 'that's where the real money is.'

'And even' – Georgiades leaned forward and whispered – 'slaves!'

'That's where the money is, too,' said the clerk. 'Or so people say,' he added hurriedly.

He wouldn't say any more, but Georgiades was satisfied for the time being. He went back to the Mamur Zapt's office at the Bab-el-Khalk and told Nikos. Nikos thought it was coming along nicely.

During the long, increasingly painful ride back to Denderah, Mahmoud had had the time to do more thinking. At first the thinking had been to do with the case. He had built so much on what he had seen as the near certainty of the clerk being able to identify the men who had come to the railway station carrying the bride box. And now it had all fallen apart! He went over it in his mind. What had gone wrong? Had the clerk simply been mistaken? Or had the men not come from the

Pasha's estate as they claimed? Had it all been an attempt to
mislead, to put an investigator on the wrong track? But from
the clerk's account of what they had said, that seemed unlikely.
He was back to the clerk again and the question of his
reliability.

He went over it again and again, getting nowhere. His
thoughts just went round and round. Had they ganged up on
him as an outsider? The city man who'd come to put the
fellahin right? Was that how they had seen him? In a way, he
could understand it if they had. But if they had, they were
being unjust. He wanted to help them. He was bringing law
into lives where the only law was that laid down by the Pasha.
Backwardness. His thinking began, in the heat and his fatigue,
to fall into familiar patterns. A man like Mustapha, for instance,
selling his own children into slavery!

It was poverty, of course. Living in Cairo, Mahmoud was
used to poverty. But what he was seeing in the south
was something new. The complete poverty in the houses!
The absolute lack of possessions – beds, even. Eating off
the floor! The very water they drank had to be carried from
the well or from the river. Even the smallest necessity cost
labour.

And even though the men worked hard in the fields, back-
breaking work under the sun, much of the work, the work that
made everything run, was done by women. Not much scope
for a life there, he thought.

He thought of Soraya seizing a few moments to put together
the things for her bride box. Every single thing had had to be
created in the few moments spared from the ordinary labour
of the house and the village.

And then he thought of the way in which those few things
had been tipped out on to the sand and scattered casually
across the desert. Life, he thought, for people like Soraya, was
pitiless. Cruel.

The thought revived the anger that burned within him when
he thought of Egypt and what Egypt had come to. He was
not, he thought, a bitter man but he felt bitter when he thought
of how the ordinary people of his country struggled. Of the
fellahin, who formed the great majority of the Egyptian

population, struggling under the oppression of the Pashas. Of Egypt as a whole struggling under the rule of foreigners. Who were the British to rule his country?

As a young boy, still at school, he had vowed to right his country's wrongs. And there were so many of them – and not just due to the British. Many were due to Egyptians themselves.

A lot of Egyptians, especially the young, thought like this. And so there was a revival of political activity, a growing feeling of the need for reform. Which is what Mahmoud, in a way, had decided to devote his life to.

Sometimes, as he never seemed to get anywhere, he felt discouraged. Why not do as others in the Parquet did and concentrate on getting rich? If you were a lawyer, there was every chance of doing that. His father would have wondered at Mahmoud. He had stinted himself to pay for his son's education, scrimped and saved so that his son would be able to do better than he had. And now his son, just when he was getting there, was addressing himself to other things! Mahmoud would have liked to debate this with him but his father was dead. But in a way he did not need his father there. He knew what he would have said.

And then there was the question of what Mahmoud's own children would say when they grew up. What would they say when all he could deliver to them was a country that could not even rule itself, that put up with the injustices and iniquities of life under the Pashas. Still! His heart burned with shame.

As he had ridden back to Denderah, his whole body aching from his long day in the saddle, his heart swimming from the sun, he had castigated himself more and more. The identification parades had been an utter failure. He had thought it would be easy. The clerk would identify the men and that would be that. But it had not turned out like that. Things weren't so simple. He blamed himself for thinking that they should have been.

And the country, too, of course. He blamed Egypt for being as backward as it was. That was the root of all the problems.

But then he came back to himself again. What had *he* done about that? Where had his political commitment got him? All the work he had put into political activity, meetings, lobbying? The Pashas were still where they had been, the British still ruled, Egypt was still . . . well, Egypt!

He felt utterly drained. He had failed again. It was all failure. Everything was failure.

Owen could have told him he was always like this. When he started on a new case, he always hit it with enthusiasm, drive. But if things went wrong, or got stuck for some reason, his thoughts would go round and round. He would get more and more depressed, feel dragged down. It would happen when he felt tired, or felt that he should have succeeded and hadn't. There was a pattern to it.

But there was another side to the pattern. At some point he would pull out of it, start to rise. He would feel buoyed up, anything would seem possible, and in no time at all he would be back to his best, driving away on top of things.

Owen had often talked about it with him. Everyone had their ups and downs, he would reassure him. It was just that he blamed himself while – said with a smile – everyone else blamed other people. This would often bring an answering, rueful smile out of Mahmoud, and would somehow start him on an upward path.

It didn't seem to do so on this occasion but, as they went on sitting there, drinking tea, Mahmoud calmed down.

After a while he jumped to his feet and said he was going to take a walk around the midan to see how much had come in since he left. This, thought Owen, was a good sign. It was positive. The low this time was not as low as it some-times could be. The other side of the pattern was activity, sometimes hyperactivity. That, at any rate, was preferable to the dreadful despondency of the low point.

As Mahmoud was wandering around he met someone he knew.

'Ya Idris!'

'Ya Mahmoud!'

They embraced joyfully.

When they had last seen each other, it had been at a political meeting in Cairo.

'What brings you here?'

'Work!'

'Oh, yes?' said Mahmoud sceptically. Idris had been a fellow student, and work had not been one of his strong points.

'No, really! These days I am into trocchee shells.'

'Trocchee shells! I never saw you as a trader!'

'I am not, really. I am hanging around with a trader in the hope that some of it will rub off on me!'

'But, Idris, down here? I thought you never went out of Cairo!'

'I don't normally. And from what I have seen of Upper Egypt, it is a policy I shall stick to in future.' He looked around mock-furtively. 'But don't let anyone know that I have said that! The lot I am with now are all for unity.'

'With Upper Egypt?'

'It gets worse: with the Sudan, too!'

'Idris, this doesn't sound like you!'

'I know. I have changed. The country has changed, too. Did you know that?'

'I must confess I hadn't spotted it.'

'Oh, yes. We're all for unity now. At least half of us are. The other half wants to go it alone. "Egypt for the Egyptians!" they say.'

'Well, we've always said that. No British, no Pashas—'

'You're thinking too narrowly, Mahmoud. What is needed is a wider unity, a unity of the Nile valley. We need to work together with our suffering brothers in the Sudan.'

'Idris, you know you can't bear to go out of Cairo . . .'

'I shall direct operations from home. Think of this foray down the Nile as an aberration. Not to be repeated.'

'You said "direct", Idris.'

'Direct, in a manner of speaking. At the moment I merely file the papers. But I shall certainly rise.'

'But, Idris, what brings you down here? This is a long way to go to file papers!'

'A foolish person has said that I will do the job better if I know what the papers are about.'

'And you come down *here* for enlightenment? Idris, are you sure you understood what they said? And, anyway, do you need to understand papers in order to file them? What,' Mahmoud said, 'are the papers about? What *could* they be about if you have to come to a place like this to find out?'

'I am not sure I should tell you, Mahmoud, you being the hireling of the Pashas that you are.'

'Look, Idris, no one down here can read or write. That rather restricts the significance of any papers that you might find to file.'

'Mahmoud,' said Idris, with dignity, 'my work is not with the fellahin, whom both you and I know to be backward and so mired in ignorance that if they rise it can only be if you and I do their thinking for them.'

'Who is it with, then?'

'As I told you, I am now a promising young member of the trading community. They trade, Mahmoud; and someone has to keep track of their tradings in case they lose track.'

'Filing the papers, you mean? But, Idris, people who trade in the desert . . .'

'Yes, but they don't trade with the people in the desert. They trade with people outside the desert. They are the only ones who can pay for what they trade in.'

'You know, Idris, I think I am beginning to get an inkling of how you feel: this sort of thing can surely be better handled from Cairo.'

'My feelings exactly, Mahmoud.'

'But I still don't see how trading in trocchee shells is going to advance the cause of the great revolution – or, if you prefer, the wider cause of the unity of the Nile valley.'

'Money, dear boy, money. Funds have to be raised, and if they are, they have to be kept track of.'

'Ye-es. But, Idris, if they have to rely on people like you to keep track, is this the position of strength that we all hope for?'

There were camels everywhere on the midan, and yet new lines of camels kept drifting in. The newcomers found it even more difficult to get a space and there were endless disputes. The camels bit and fought. Big ones shouldered smaller ones aside, butted and snarled. The drivers waded in with whips to restore order. Eventually it was restored, and the camels were hobbled and settled down. This didn't usually happen until they had been watered and forage brought. The forage, usually green clover, was spread on the ground in front of them. Then they set to at once. As they chewed, a green dribble ran out of the sides of their mouths and soon the whole midan was covered with a green mess. It was like one continuous green cowpat.

Mahmoud picked his steps fastidiously. It was probably wise to do that anyway. You needed to give camels a wide berth. When they were standing they would sometimes lash out with a foot which had enough force to break your leg. They were unruly, surly, savage beasts; not at all like cows.

Gradually he began to make sense of the melee in the square. Incoming loads were deposited on the station side. The sacks of gum arabic were piled alongside the railway line, ready for loading. Further back, waiting their turn, were the sacks of trocchee shells. Sometimes the sacks were torn and you would see the shells spilling out. They had a strong fishy smell.

Further back still, because they were of less importance, were bags of goods for the bazaars of the south, on their way to the shops of the Sudan. And here and there were little piles of private belongings, to be picked up when everything else was out of the way.

Everywhere, too, were the Levantine assistants of the traders, conspicuous among the galabeyas in their white shirts and European-style trousers, running from pile to pile, papers in hand, counting this pile, ticking off that.

The midan now surged with people and camels. Despite himself, Mahmoud was impressed. He had never anticipated a gathering of this scale in such an obscure part of the desert. Everywhere was hubbub and bustle.

As he threaded his way through the mass, he was surprised to see the Pasha's lady's son, Karim. He had never expected to see him so far from home.

He was wandering around with a dazed expression on his face, As Mahmoud watched him, he ran into someone he knew.

'Ya Hassan!'

'Ya Karim! Are you well?'

'Well, thanks be to God! And you?'

'Well also.'

'Are you coming to see me?'

'Perhaps.'

'I am hoping that you would be bringing something for me.'

Hassan smiled. 'Well, I was hoping you might be bringing something for *me*!'

'It's on the way. Tamuz is bringing it.'

'More than one box, I hope?'

'All those you left. Six donkeys.'

'Six?'

'Two boxes on each donkey and one over.'

'Those boxes are heavy. It is a lot for a donkey to carry.'

'You should have sent camels.'

Hassan shrugged. 'They couldn't be spared. However, as long as the boxes are here to go with the others . . .'

'They will be here tomorrow, Tamuz says.'

'God be praised!'

'And is there anything for me?'

Hassan smiled and patted him familiarly on the shoulder. 'There is a fine new gun. And I know it's fine because I have seen it fired. It brought down a hawk. At two hundred paces!'

'That was a good shot!'

'It was I who fired it. But, yes, it was. And the gun is a good one. It is like some of those in the boxes. It has new sights on it. You won't have seen them before, but they are astonishing. You will find a difference at once.'

'Can I have it?' asked Karim excitedly.

'When the boxes get in.'

'Not until then?' said Karim, disappointed.

'Not until then. But then at once. You will have the new gun with you when you go with Tamuz. I promise you!'

Hassan moved away. Karim looked around uncertainly for a moment and then moved off too. Mahmoud waited for him to go and then went in search of Owen.

\*   \*   \*

Owen walked back to the carpenter's shop.

'Can I borrow Selim?'

'Of course!'

'It will be for a day or two.'

'That's all right. We're not busy.'

Owen went over to Selim, who was working quietly in the back of the shop. 'Selim, I need your help.'

'Anything I can do, Effendi . . .'

'It is not an ordinary thing I am asking you for.'

Selim looked at him quickly. 'Is it to do with Soraya?'

'Indirectly, yes.'

'Then I will help.'

'Let us go to the temple.'

They clambered their way through the sunken nitre tanks and went into the temple. They stood for a moment in its cold gloom. The slightly musty air met him again. They waited for their eyes to get used to the darkness and then went through to the room Selim had shown him before. Nothing seemed to have changed in it.

'It will,' said Owen. 'I think they plan to use it.'

'To store . . .?'

'As they have done before. When they come, I want you to be here but not seen.'

'I will not be seen.'

'I will come to you from time to time. But I must not be seen either. I will bring you food and water.'

'Food and water?'

'You will need them. You may be here for a day or two. Not longer, I think. But I need to know when the men come. Then come to me.'

'You will seize them?'

'Not yet. I think they will be bringing guns. And I need to know when the guns leave.'

'I will tell you, Effendi.'

'Take no risk.'

Selim thought for a moment. 'Effendi, is not the greater risk that you yourself will be seen when you come?'

'I shall take care.'

'Effendi, when you come, come as the English usually do,

to look at the temple. Stand in front of the marks as if perusing them. I shall whistle like this.' He imitated the mew of a hawk. 'When you hear that, come into the temple. I shall be waiting behind the pillars.'

The clerk was not yet back at the station. His brother, however, was still standing in for him. He greeted Owen warmly.

'Your duties grow,' said Owen.

'I should be paid more,' said the clerk's brother.

'But so does the need for silence.'

'I can be silent.'

'It is important that no one hears of this. If they do, expect the Khedive's wrath.'

'The Khedive need have no fears.'

'I am expecting some boxes to come to the station. Heavy boxes. They will not be easy to lift. There will be men with them. They will put them on the train. When that happens, I need to know.'

'You will know, Effendi.'

Mahmoud wandered through the goods piled along the railway line.

'What is it, Effendi, that you look for?'

'I see only gum arabic.'

'That is what we deal in.'

'I am told there would be trocchee shells.'

'Ah, yes. Those we have, too. But first we have to load the gum arabic. When we get that out of the way, we can load the trocchee shells.'

'Will that not take time?'

'It will.'

'The trocchee shells will have to wait for another train, perhaps?'

'Perhaps. There is a lot of gum arabic to shift.'

'The shells may even have to wait for another day?'

'They may. With the shells, it does not matter.'

'I am also expecting some boxes. Heavy boxes, which will require much lifting. When will they be put on the train?'

'It depends when they come.'

'Some are already here. But others arrive, I think, tomorrow.'

'Who brings them?'

'Tamuz. I think.'

'Ah, yes. Tamuz. Yes, I think he comes tomorrow.'

'But some of the boxes are already here?'

'That is so, Effendi. Most of them are already here. The ones Tammy brings are but a small part.'

'It is a big load, then.'

'A big load, as you say, Effendi.'

'But all is in hand, then, is it?'

'All is in hand, Effendi.'

The next day, at noon, when the sun was at its hottest and the huge encampment was still, Selim came running.

'The men, Effendi!'

'They have come?'

This first visit had obviously been in the nature of a reconnaissance. A man had come and nosed around. He had gone inside, Selim thought to the back of the temple, probably to the chamber he had pointed out to Owen. Then he had come out and stood waiting and then another man had joined him and they had both gone inside. Apparently what they had seen had satisfied them for, said Selim, they had both looked pleased when they reappeared.

They had stood there talking for a little while longer and Selim had crept forward behind the columns to eavesdrop. What they were discussing was speed. How quickly could it be done? They had wanted to be sure that it would not take long.

The first man had assured the other man it wouldn't. The donkeys could be brought right up to the temple and even inside. They wouldn't be exposed to the risk of being seen for more than a couple of minutes. The boxes could be unloaded and taken to the chamber. And if they were brought when it was getting dark the chance of being observed was even less. They could do their business and then slip away again undetected.

The second man had remained uneasy. 'I don't like this,' he said. 'Are they good marks? Or the work of the Devil? I mean, this place is . . . It's not exactly holy, is it?'

'It wasn't holy when they built it. It was built in the days of the Giants and they didn't know God's word. Our people came along later and sort of took it over. The old caravans used to pass close to here, at Kuft. And what I reckon happened was that they looked at this place and thought it ought to be made decent. So they painted our signs up there.'

'Yes, but are they our signs?'

'Oh, yes. You can see that. There's the moon and the stars – all the signs of the heavens! The work of the sages.'

'In line with the Koran?'

'Oh, definitely!'

'This must be a holy place, then.'

'Oh, it is. That's what I've been telling you. Put up by our holy men to show that the place was now decent. And that means it's all right for us to put our things here.'

'I suppose it does, yes.'

'And at the same time it keeps people off.'

'Well, it would.'

'Giants *and* sages! That's a pretty powerful combination.'

'I'm not that keen on it myself.'

'That's just my point. No one is. So the boxes will be all right.'

'Has the boss seen it?'

'Came here himself just to take a look.'

'And he thought it was OK?

'Just the place,' he said. Mind you, there was a bit of a worry. There was a kid around when he came and he didn't like that. He worried that she might have seen something or heard something. But Ali said, "What could she have seen? There weren't any boxes here then." "Yes, but she might have heard something," says the boss. "What could she have heard?" asked Ali. "And would she have understood anything?"

'But the boss still fretted about it. He's like that, you know. Worries about everything. Doesn't like to leave anything to chance. Wanted to know who this girl was. "Maybe we ought to do something about her," he said. I think, as a matter of fact, he *did* do something about her.'

'He didn't . . .?'

'No. Just saw that she was taken care of. But then it went wrong somehow. And now he's worried about her again. Thinks we ought to do something. We're supposed to be keeping an eye out for her.'

'Well, I haven't seen any signs of a kid.'

'Nor have I. But I'm just telling you. In case you do see her.'

# EIGHT

Mahmoud's daughter, Maryam, went to school. This was uncommon even among his colleagues at the Parquet. Having themselves got where they were by education, they were all in favour of it for their own young. For their sons, that was. Even among the relatively liberal Parquet lawyers, valuing of education and ambition for their offspring did not extend as far as educating their daughters, too.

Or in any case, only a bit. When their daughters grew old enough for their fathers to notice their existence and to start planning for their marriages a few of them were sent to special European-style finishing schools so that they might not be totally boring to their husbands when they got married, who were also likely to be bright Parquet lawyers.

Mahmoud, however, thought differently. Only the best was going to be good enough for *his* children, male or female, and he meant to see that right from the start they received an education along progressive Western lines. There were in Cairo one or two kindergartens chiefly for the children of well-to-do Europeans. It was to one of these that he decided to send Maryam.

When he learned what it was going to cost him he almost changed his mind. Young Parquet lawyers, no matter how bright, were not highly paid. Aisha, however, his strong-willed and equally liberal wife, who was just becoming aware of some of the arguments about the 'New Woman' that were currently occurring in France, did not agree. Equality of the sexes had to begin very early – indeed, from birth – and her adored Maryam was certainly going to receive as good an education as any brother.

Mahmoud, logical to the last, had to admit the force of this point of view: so Maryam went, hand in hand with her mother, to the kindergarten every morning.

And where she went, could not Leila go too? Or so Zeinab thought. Aisha was not sure about this. Leila was an adorable child, but was she as capable of benefiting from advanced education in the way that her own perfect daughter certainly would be able to?

And then there was the question of cost. Owen was barely richer than Mahmoud and Leila, damn it, was not even their daughter. Zeinab hadn't the faintest idea about money except that she knew Owen hadn't got any; so she applied, as she usually did, to her father. Nuri Pasha didn't know much about money either – he left all that sort of thing to his steward – but he did know that he had less than he thought he did. However, he was interested in the latest French fashions when it came to ideas. He had brought up Zeinab very much *au courant* with them and had made no difference between her and his son, a decision much assisted by the fact that he couldn't help noticing that Zeinab was about twice as bright as her brother.

So he saw no reason why Leila shouldn't be educated, and the fact that she was the next best thing to a slave's daughter was no problem to him. Hadn't Zeinab's own mother started off as a slave? And she had developed into the most beautiful courtesan in Cairo. It may be that Leila could do the same! She was a bright little girl, according to Zeinab. Why not? Stranger things had happened. So he didn't mind paying for Leila to go to the kindergarten; it could even be looked upon as an investment.

So off now went Leila every morning, hand in hand with Maryam, usually with Aisha or Zeinab but sometimes with Musa's wife in attendance.

The warehouse clerk and the Greek were by now great buddies. Rare was the morning when Georgiades did not drop in to take the clerk round the corner to the coffee house they favoured. The clerk felt that he was doing the Greek a good turn by lending a sympathetic ear to his tales of marital woe; and, besides, as he confessed to Georgiades, there wasn't much happening in the warehouse at the moment. 'But it will all be different next week,' he said.

'How's that?'

'Well, Clarke Effendi is returning and bringing with him many goods, which will all have to be put in their right places and accounted for – and, no doubt, there will soon be billing to be done.'

'Bales and bales of gum arabic?' said the Greek. 'And trocchee shells?'

'And other things, too.'

'Pretty slave girls?' prompted Georgiades.

'I should be so lucky!' said the clerk. He shook his head. 'No,' he said, 'no such luck. But sometimes there is a special consignment.' He put up his hand. 'Don't ask me what it is,' he said. 'I don't know. Clarke Effendi keeps all that to himself.' He laid a finger along his nose. 'He handles it all himself. Everything! The goods come in and then go out and neither I nor anyone else is allowed to go near them. Nor even the paperwork. *Especially* not the paperwork. Clarke Effendi does it all. "The less you know about it, the better," he says. "If you don't know anything, you can't tell anyone anything. It's better like that." And,' said the clerk, 'I think it is better. Because the old bastard is up to something, you can be sure. And the less I know about it, the better.'

'There is wisdom,' said the Greek admiringly. 'It's a wise man who knows when it's best not to know something!'

'Of course, I have to know a bit,' said the warehouse clerk. 'I have to know when a consignment like that is coming in, so that I can make space for it. And it's not just any sort of space; it's got to be over in a corner, where people don't come upon it by mischance. And it's got to be in the usual place in case he wants to move it by dark. In fact, he usually does want to move it by dark. That's another thing, you see. What people don't see, they don't think about, he says.

'But once or twice I've had to be there to see to the moving – make sure the right boxes are collected. It would never do to have the wrong box picked up. And that would be easy to do in the dark. Of course, we've got torches, but still, it helps if someone who knows about it is there to see to it. Actually, he likes to see to that himself. Never trusts anybody else when it's important. I suppose that's why he does so well. Why he's a rich man and I am not!'

'There are costs to being rich,' said the Greek. 'That's what I always tell my wife. You've got to be thinking about your money all the time.'

'The risk!' said the warehouse clerk.

'Suppose it went wrong?' said the Greek.

'Ah, then you're in trouble!' said the clerk.

'I'll bet you didn't say that to Clarke Effendi, though!'

'You'd win your bet!' said the clerk. 'That's another thing he says. "No silly questions, no sharp answers!"'

'And that's true, too,' said the Greek.

'Still, there are things that I know and that he doesn't know. How to get hold of a reliable porter in Cairo, for example.'

'Can't trust the buggers!' said the Greek.

'You've got to stand over them. And although he'd prefer to do that himself, that's not always possible.'

'So you have to do it?'

'That's it!'

'Even at night!'

'Even at night. Especially at night!'

'Because of the temptation to wander off and have a drink?'

'He'd go mad!'

'I'll bet he would. But that's what they'd do if you weren't standing right behind them.'

'You can't afford for it to go wrong.'

'Not when there's a Pasha involved.'

'Oh, so that's the way the land lies, is it? I don't envy you.'

'Just occasionally. I don't do it every time, of course, and I don't know about the other times. But I know what I know.'

'And you're not saying!' said the Greek, chuckling.

'Too true, I'm not!'

'Well I think he's a lucky man to have you to call on.'

'Well, I think he is, too. It's not easy to get things done the way he likes them done. There's more to it than he thinks. Just getting the stuff here is not that straightforward. It comes in by train, you see, and has to be fetched from the station. Nothing to it, you might think. Just a matter of porters. But porters have to be found, and porters have to be stood over, like I said, or else they'll get it wrong. And then he'd go mad!'

'Do you use the same porters every time?'

'Why do you ask?'

'I should think you would. If he's like you say, you'd want to be sure of your porters. And if you've found some you know to be reliable, I think you'd stick with them.'

'Well, I do, as a matter of fact.'

'Go to the same ones every time?'

'That's right.'

'I reckon you've done well if you've found some reliable ones.'

'It's not easy. In a place like Cairo. Where porters are always drifting away. Offer them some money and they're off!'

'Does he pay well?'

'No.'

Georgiades pursed his lips. 'That makes it tricky,' he said.

'It does. That's what I always tell him. "You don't know the half of it," I say.'

'He's a lucky man to have you to rely on.'

Further along the street was a barber's shop. Well, not quite a shop – this was a poor area – but certainly a barber. He worked from the pavement, where he had put a chair, an old cane chair, on which he sat his clients. His equipment was on the ground beside him: two pairs of scissors, one for hard work, the other for fine: a razor, of the cut-throat variety, a shaving brush, a tin bowl and a large pewter jug containing the hot water he had to fetch from the café up the road where Georgiades and the warehouse clerk went for their coffee. And there was a length of cloth, not overly clean, which he tied round the neck of his client. From time to time he shook it into the gutter.

There was always a circle of onlookers gathered round the chair, sitting on the pavement, offering advice or critical judgement or just generally chatting. The barber was good at chatting and the people who came to join him were regulars. Some passed the day there.

The Greek ambled along the street, paused when he saw the barber and hovered uncertainly. The chair was empty at the moment and the barber spread his apron cloth invitingly. Georgiades sat down. 'Short back and sides,' he said.

'It's pretty short already,' said the barber doubtfully. 'Are you sure you want a haircut?'

'My wife says I need one.'

'Perhaps she was thinking of your beard?'

'I haven't got one!' protested Georgiades.

'Maybe that's the problem. You've got a lot of stubble there.'

'My hair grows quickly!'

'It does on some people.'

'I shave every morning, you know, and by ten o'clock it looks as if I haven't touched it.'

'It's the jowls – they hide the hair, and you can't cut closely, and then as the day wears on, the hairs come back from behind the flesh.'

'This is getting personal!' said Georgiades.

'No, no, it's just a technical observation. I'm right, aren't I?' he appealed to the onlookers.

'It's true he's a bit fleshy,' one observer piped up.

'I can't help that!'

'No, he can't. And stop going on at him. Some people carry a lot of weight. It's the way they are.'

'It's certainly the way I am,' said Georgiades.

'All he needs is a shave!' someone else shouted.

'You could be right,' said the barber.

'All right, a shave, then.'

'Go on,' the crowd advised. 'Make it nice for his wife. She doesn't want to be scraping herself against his bristles all the time. That's the problem. It's not his hair.'

'A shave, then,' said the barber. 'As smooth as a baby's bottom.'

After this promising beginning, the conversation flowed, and soon the Greek was in a position to ask about the porters.

'Reliable ones,' he stipulated.

'You'll be lucky!'

'I know, but a chap who works in one of the warehouses here was telling me that he reckoned he'd found some.'

'All the warehouses use porters!'

'Yes, but some are better than others. This bloke I was talking to seemed to need especially good ones. He worked for a foreign Effendi, you see, who was always on to him.'

'Would that be Nassir?'

'It might be. I didn't quite catch his name. But he said he worked for a foreign Effendi who was often away – a trader. Gum arabic, I think. And trocchee shells.'

'That definitely was Nassir.'

'Why do his porters have to be so special?' asked someone. 'That's just ordinary work.'

'Sometimes they have to move stuff at night,' said Georgiades. 'And then, I suppose they're working without supervision.'

'Why do they have to move the stuff at night?'

'God knows! But apparently they do. Anyway it sounded as if he'd got some good porters, and I just wondered if anyone knew who they were? Because I could certainly use them.'

'They come from outside, I think.'

He meant outside the quarter. Cairo was a very localized place as far as ordinary people were concerned.

'They do mostly,' said someone. 'But I think he makes use of Abdul.'

'Well, Abdul is very good. If you want someone who's reliable, he's your man.'

'How could I get hold of him?'

'You'll find him just along the road. At the trough there. When he's not working, that is, which is most of the time.'

Yet further along the road was another business conducted entirely on the pavement. It consisted of a large flat tray resting on a layer of cinders and filled with cooking oil, usually olive or sunflower. Beside the tray was a cloth on which were lying various pieces of meat and sundry vegetables. From time to time its attendant would drop a piece of meat or a few vegetables into the cooking fat. They would sizzle and turn brown. When they were done he would fish them out and hand them, usually on a piece of paper, to whoever had requested them. Then they would sit on the pavement and eat them.

For this was a restaurant. It did not cater for the exalted (it was not even like the place Georgiades and the warehouse clerk attended just along the road) but for porters, donkey-boys, warehouse workers and the humbler men who did menial jobs round about. And, like the barber's shop, it was a humming social centre.

Georgiades stood over the tray, obviously tempted. The smell of frying onions rose enticingly into the air.

'Try some!' invited the cook.

Georgiades sat down. The cook ladled some onion slices on to a square of paper and put it in front of Georgiades.

'Yes?' said the cook anxiously.

'Yes,' said Georgiades, and handed the square back for more.

'And something else?'

'Aubergines?' said Georgiades hopefully.

The cook pointed. 'In the pot,' he said.

Georgiades held out the square.

'And . . .?' said the cook.

'Beans.'

'Beans, yes. And . . .?'

Georgiades held up his hand. 'No more,' he said. 'My wife says I eat too much anyway.'

'How could she say that?' said the cook, affecting amazement. 'A slim fellow like you!'

'That's what I say. But somehow she's not convinced.'

There were several other men squatting around the tray. They pointed out, in the friendly, intimate Egyptian way, the best aubergines and helped him to extract them from the pot.

'One thing I do like,' said Georgiades, 'is a good aubergine! With onions, of course. They're good for you, did you know that?'

'Of course they're good for you!' said the cook. 'They keep headaches off.'

'I find they're good for my back,' said one of the customers.

There was some discussion about this.

'You need onions if you're a porter,' said the Greek.

'You do,' various people assented.

'Talking of porters,' said the Greek, 'is Abdul here, by any chance?'

A man raised his hand. He had a great strap round his shoulders to assist carrying.

'You look a big, fine fellow,' said the Greek.

The porter grinned. 'What is it this time?' he said. 'A piano?'

'I'll bet you could manage it.'

'I could.'

He meant single-handed.

'I'll be back for you!' said Georgiades.

In fact, someone else called for Abdul, and off he went.

Later in the afternoon, however, he returned. The Greek had eaten a lot of aubergines by that time and had gone away. But he was standing at the edge of the little square, from where he could keep an eye on the pavement restaurant, and when Abdul reappeared, he went up to him and suggested a beer. Strictly speaking, as a good Muslim, he shouldn't touch alcohol, but, as he said, in his job you needed a lot of liquid, so he went off with Georgiades around the corner.

'I could have a job for you,' said the Greek. 'It's a big one, and there's big money in it. For a good porter. A reliable man who knows how to keep his mouth shut.'

'Big money, did you say?'

The Greek nodded.

'I'm not a fussy man,' said Abdul.

'It might mean working at night.'

'One of those, is it?'

'Well, you know how it is. These rich men don't want their right hand to know what their left is doing!'

'I can keep my mouth shut.'

'That's important.'

'Carpets, is it?'

'Heavier.'

'No problem.'

'The thing is, my boss insists that his porters have got to be absolutely reliable.'

'He can rely on me,' said Abdul.

'He likes recommended people. Your name was mentioned

to me by someone who manages a warehouse near here. Nassir, his name was . . .'

'I know Nassir.'

'You've done jobs for him before, I gather?'

'I have.'

'He says he might be needing you in the next few days. I wouldn't want to clash with him. I mean, he'd done me a favour by putting me on to you. So just tell me, will you, when his job comes up? And I'll see we keep clear of it. I'll be around here for a while, so I'll be sticking my head in at the eats place and you can tell me there.'

Owen and Mahmoud were walking across the midan when they ran into Karim. Mahmoud introduced them. 'This is my friend, Captain Owen,' he said.

'Hello!' said Karim. 'Pleased to meet you. Are you really a captain?'

'Well, I was,' said Owen. 'But not now.'

'Have you given it up?'

'Yes, that's right. I've given it up. Some time ago, actually.'

'Does that mean you were a soldier?'

'Yes. In India.'

'India,' said Karim uncertainly. 'Where is that? Is it near Cairo?'

'A long way away from Cairo, actually. It's over the sea. You'd have to go on a ship.'

'I've never been on a ship,' said Karim. 'But I've been in a boat. On the river.'

'It's like that,' said Owen. 'Only the sea is much, much bigger.'

'I would like to go on the sea.'

'Perhaps one day you will.'

Karim contemplated the prospect. But then the distance in time and space was too much for him. He lost interest. His attention was caught by the parcel Owen was carrying. 'What is that parcel?' he asked.

'It is a present,' said Owen. 'A present for a little girl.'

'Can I see it?'

Owen unwrapped it.

'I know what it is,' said Karim. 'It's a box.' He took it from

Owen and fondled it. 'It is a nice box,' he said. 'All smooth.'
He stroked it, thinking. 'I know what it is!' he said suddenly.
'It is a box like Soraya had. Only smaller, much smaller.'

'It is a plaything only,' said Owen.

Karim nodded. 'Yes,' he said, 'for a child. But it is like
Soraya's box. Only smaller. She showed me her box once,
you know. She opened it and let me look in. There were all
sorts of nice things in it. Things she had made. There was a
little . . .'

He stopped, and frowned.

'A little thing,' he said. 'I don't know its name. It was a
little patch of cloth. Only about this wide.' He indicated with
his hands. 'And soft, very soft. She let me feel it. She said
she would make me one. I wanted her to make me one.' He
imitated putting it to his face. 'So soft,' he said. 'So soft.
Like Soraya.'

'Like Soraya?'

'Soft,' said Karim, 'so soft.'

'You touched her?'

'She let me touch her. She let me hold her hand. It was very
nice. And when she touched me – she touched my face – her
hand was so soft. So gentle! No one had ever touched me like
that before. I said that. I told her that. And . . . and she cried!
I don't know why she cried! Do you know why she cried?'

'I can guess,' said Owen.

'It was a little square,' Karim said. 'She had sewn it herself.
There were little beads on it. They were made of glass and
they sparkled in the sun. It was lovely. I asked her to make
me one, and she said she would. I wonder what has happened
to it. They have taken all her things away, you know. When
she left. With the box.'

'Did you see her go?'

'No. It happened one night. After I had gone to bed. She
left, and she took her box with her. And that little thing – I
don't know what you call it – must have been inside. And
I don't think she ever made one for me. Or perhaps she did?
And it's lying around somewhere. I'll ask my mother if she's
seen it.'

\*    \*    \*

'Pity me, Mahmoud!'

It was his old friend from student days.

'Willingly; but why should I pity you, Idris?'

'I told you a lie yesterday, Mahmoud.'

'One of many, I am sure; but which one specifically?'

'I told you I was a trader in trocchee shells.'

'And are you not?'

'Oh, I am. But also I am not.'

'But that is not a lie, Idris. That is merely a half-truth.'

'Put it another way, Mahmoud: I have not one job, but two.'

'But, Idris, this is astonishing. Two jobs! And are both of them paid? You must be on your way to riches!'

'I should be so lucky! I am barely paid enough for one.'

'It will build up, Idris, I am sure.'

'But slowly. And the trouble is, Mahmoud, that there is no gain without pain.'

'You have to work for it?'

'Worse. A consignment has just arrived. And when it arrives, it has to be split.'

'That is not an insurmountable problem, Idris.'

'And I have to split it.'

'It is still not insurmountable, Idris. Challenging, possibly, but not impossible.'

'One part has to go to Cairo. The other to the Sudan.'

'Difficult, but not—'

'And I have to go with it.'

'To the Sudan?'

'If it was to Cairo, there would be no problem.'

'Still . . .'

'The Sudan, Mahmoud, the Sudan! Where giant scorpions lie in waiting. And lizards as large as crocodiles. And *flies*, Mahmoud, flies in abundance!'

'But are you not used to flies?'

'Not flies like these. They are cannibal flies, Mahmoud. They consume you.'

'Not flies, Idris, not flies!'

'Mosquitoes, then. Truly malignant ones. The sort that give you malaria by a stab. And the sand, Mahmoud, and the heat.

Where the water, if there is any, runs already hot from the taps! I shall die, Mahmoud, I shall die!'

'Again, Idris, I wonder if you have completely understood. Are you sure you have to send part of the consignment to the Sudan? Is not the Sudan where trocchee shells come from, not go to?'

'I am not talking about trocchee shells.'

'No? What are you talking about, then?'

'That, I cannot reveal to you.'

'All right, be like that, then!'

'I told you I have two jobs. The trocchee shells are one. This is another.'

'So it is not trocchee shells that you are dividing?'

'No. Mahmoud, it does not matter what I am dividing. *I don't want to go to the Sudan!*'

'Why go, then?

'Duty.'

'Oh, come, Idris!'

'You and I both serve a great ideal, Mahmoud. Duty calls. In a hell-hole like the Sudan, the call is muted, I will allow: but it is still there. I wish it weren't. Oh, how I wish it weren't!'

'Have courage, man; you may return alive.'

'Or I may not.'

'Whereabouts in the Sudan are you bound for?'

'I don't know, exactly. Somewhere between the Red Sea Hills and Port Sudan. Between the Devil and the deep sea, Mahmoud. Both are equally undesirable.'

'Well, Idris, when you get there, will you send me a post-card, so that I will know where to come to collect your body?'

'Mahmoud, is it even *possible* to send postcards in the Sudan?'

'Of course it is. There is a very good postal service there.'

'I will send you one, then. In fact, I will send you more than one. So that you will know that my life still flickers.'

As Mahmoud walked away, he felt slightly uncomfortable. If Idris did send him a postcard, he would know where Idris had gone – and, presumably, where his part of the consignment had gone, too.

Did that matter? Mahmoud rather feared that it did. Because

what was this mysterious consignment? It couldn't be ordinary goods, or Idris would have said. It was something he had to be guarded about. So what could it be?

Mahmoud had an uneasy suspicion that it might be arms. Idris appeared to have been sent on some sort of political mission. He had always been a bit of a hot-head. At university he had always taken up extreme positions. Well, was that so bad? reflected Mahmoud. So had he himself. So had most students.

But Idris had always carried them further than most of their friends, had talked more wildly, had always been in the forefront of demonstration against the government. But that was just Idris. Except that Idris had gone on for longer, had gone on after he had left university, when most others had let themselves be swallowed up by work. They had sunk into respectable, responsible jobs – as Mahmoud had himself. True, he had kept the ideal burning bright, had constantly worked for it in his off-duty moments. But that was not quite the same as devoting your life to it full-time. Idris had committed himself totally to the cause and gone on committing himself. You shouldn't let yourself be fooled by his flippant manner. Idris wasn't the fool he sometimes pretended to be.

This business that he was presently engaged in, whatever it was, was serious. There could be no doubt about that. And it was, of course, political.

Nothing wrong with that, in Mahmoud's eyes. Except . . . except that a lot depended on *how* it was political. If it was violent, Mahmoud didn't like it. He had a distaste for any form of terrorist or quasi-terrorist activity. Well, he would, wouldn't he, as a member of the Parquet. He wanted change but he wanted it to come by peaceful means. He was used, of course, to being accused of siding with the Pashas and the British. And there was, he had to recognize, some truth in the change. But, committed as he was to change, he was also committed to the law. That, after all, was why he had chosen to become a lawyer. He believed that through the law his vision of a better Egypt could be accomplished. Through politics, yes, but above all through the law. Politics in the end had to be subject to the law. And he knew that too often in Egypt it wasn't.

He had thought it through over and over and had arrived at a position which satisfied him. But every now and then something cropped up which jarred it. As now. Should he follow up what Idris had let slip and see if there really was something questionable, illegal, in what he was doing? And did it matter if there was? There were lots of things that for an Egyptian official it was convenient not to know. Was he making too much of this? Should he not just forget about it?

He knew what the worldly wise Owen would say: at least wait for the postcard!

# NINE

There were still camel trains coming in, although less frequently, and smaller ones now. When they reached the midan they came to a halt while their drivers tried to find a space for them. When this failed they sometimes tried to force their way in among the camels already there. Often the camels resisted and bit and lashed out with their hind legs at the newcomers. Then the camel herds would rush in with their whips and try to restore order. There were bitter arguments.

Owen was hovering around, keeping an eye on new arrivals when he saw Karim again. This time he was carrying a gun.

'That's a fine gun!' said Owen.

'It is, isn't it?' said Karim proudly. 'It's one of the new ones, with the new improved sights.'

'May I look?'

It was one of the new service rifles, which were only just being issued to the army. Owen wondered how it had been obtained. He squinted through the new sights.

'Be careful!' said Karim anxiously.

'It's not loaded, is it?'

'No, but my mother says you've got to be very careful with guns. No loaded guns in the house! Nor anywhere where there are people. That's the rule and she's very strict about it. It's been the rule ever since Ibrahim died.'

'Ibrahim?'

'From my mother's side of the family. He used to come up and see my father a lot. That was when we lived in the old house. And when he came he used to let me play with his gun. Well, one day I was playing with it, when it went off. And Ibrahim fell down. And then . . .'

He stopped.

'And then?' prompted Owen.

Karim looked puzzled. 'I don't remember,' he said. 'I don't

always remember things. My mother says I must try harder. It's important, she says. And I do remember some things. But I don't remember others. I do remember, though, that Ibrahim fell down. And then my mother took the gun away from me. I cried, but she said I was too small. So she took it away and made the rule. No guns in the house!'

'A very sensible rule,' said Owen. 'But what about Ibrahim?'

'I don't remember. He didn't come to the house again. He fell down. And perhaps he was put in a box? Or was it someone else who was put in a box? I think he was just wrapped up. I don't remember. But my father was very angry and said I had to go. And my mother said it wasn't my fault. Ibrahim ought to have known better. And she said that if I went she would go with me.

'So she and I went to the other house. And my father went away up to Cairo. And Ibrahim stopped coming. But sometimes people do come up from the Sudan still. Only, of course, it's no good them going to the old house these days. My father's not there. So they come to us. My mother likes to see them and have a good chat. About the family and that sort of thing. And then she sends them away. I don't know where to. Perhaps to Cairo? I think they want to see my father. There's a lot of business to do. Only now, of course, they have to go up to Cairo, which is much further for them, and they don't like it. My mother says it would be better if my father came down here. But he won't. I think it may be because of me.'

'That would be a pity,' said Owen.

'That is what Soraya said. And my mother was very angry, and said that a Pasha did not need to take instruction from a servant girl.'

A man came up at that point and spoke to Karim. He gestured at the gun. 'Better let me have that,' he said.

'I want to keep it,' said Karim sulkily.

'Tamuz says, let him keep it. He will give it to you on the way home.'

'Ah!' said Owen. 'So Tamuz is here now?'

The man looked at him coolly.

'Yes,' he said, 'Tamuz is here.'

'And the boxes?'

'I don't know anything about boxes,' said the man.

Mahmoud set off early the next morning, while it was still dark, for the Pasha's lady's house. Riding in the cool made it much more pleasant and the journey did not seem so long this time. By the time it grew light he was nearly at the house and able to find the last part of the way easily.

'You are back,' said the Pasha's lady.

'The police are always back,' said Mahmoud, 'when they have not been told correctly when they first came.'

The lady raised her eyebrows.

'What is this?' she said.

'You did not tell me all,' said Mahmoud.

'All?' said the lady bitterly. 'That would be a long story!'

'And you took care that I should not hear it,' said Mahmoud. 'You sent Suleiman away.'

'I sent Suleiman away because I had work for him to do. Do you think the world stops for you, Mr Parquet man?'

'I wished to see him. With the others.'

'You will have to wait, then. For he is with my family in the Sudan. And will not come back until I tell him to.'

'That is disappointing,' said Mahmoud. 'Because this is an important matter.'

'Is it to do with that girl?'

'Yes.'

'Then that is not important. She was merely a servant girl.'

'To be commanded,' said Mahmoud. 'But not to be killed.'

'The men who killed her are, no doubt, evil men; but not without wit.'

'Why do you say that?'

'Because they sent her to my husband.'

'Wit?'

'She was a Sudani. And he loves Sudanis. Doesn't he?'

'He loved you once.'

'And then he didn't any more.'

'Are you saying he loved someone else? A Sudani?'

'It may be, for all I know.'

'Soraya?'

She startled. 'Soraya! He might have used her. But I don't think he would have *loved* her. She was just a servant girl.'

'I wondered why you sent her away?'

'Not because of my husband, I assure you!' said the lady drily. 'I would lay many charges against him, but not that!'

'Why did you send her away?'

'She was presumptuous. She presumed too much.'

'In what way?'

She was silent. Then she said: 'I prefer not to tell you.'

'Presumptuous, I would accept as a reason for dismissal from your service. But I would like an instance of it.'

'She brought her bride box.'

'But that was the second time that she came. What of the first?'

'There were indications,' she said, after a moment.

'Indications? Of what?' He waited. 'You will have to tell me in the end. Was it Karim?'

'Perhaps,' she said.

'You will have to tell me.'

She was silent, Then: 'Karim is . . . backward. In all things. In this as in other things. He did not understand what she was doing to him. I had to protect him.'

'So you sent her away?'

'I had to end it.'

'But then you decided not to. You called her back.' ·

'I was foolish. It was ended. I should have let it stay like that. But . . . he missed her. I could see that. A mother knows. He became difficult. The heart went out of him. I thought it would go away, but it didn't. So I thought . . .'

She made an impatient gesture with her hand, as if sweeping it away. 'I thought, perhaps after all it was for the good. Or could be for the good if I could control it. If she gave him pleasure, well, why not? There was not much pleasure in his life. And she was kind to him, I could see that. And gradually in him something stirred. I could see that, too. And in a way I rejoiced at it. Do not laugh at me. I was foolish, I know. But a mother of a child like mine always hopes – can't *not* hope – that perhaps by some miracle her son will become a man. A foolish hope in the case of Karim, I know, but . . . but you

can't help hoping. And it seemed to be happening, because of
Soraya. So . . . so I sent for her again. Hoping that . . . but
knowing inside that . . .' She made the gesture again, fiercely.
'I was foolish. As I have said.'

'You found you could not control it?'

'Who can control these things?'

Again the gesture: dismissal, but also despair.

'And Soraya, too, perhaps, was foolish?' suggested
Mahmoud. 'For she, too, had hopes.'

'She set her hopes too high. They were not realistic. What
would Karim's father, his father's family, have said? A Pasha's
son and a servant girl! And what – given the way that Karim
was – what might they bring into the family? Another monster?
That is how he, and they, would have seen it. Another monster
to begin, perhaps, a line of monsters. No, I could not let this
happen. I could not do that, even to my husband! So I sent
her away again. And broke Karim's heart.'

'You sent them both away. Her and the bride box?'

'I thought of sending just the box away. I thought that would
be a sign. Would tell her what she needed to realize. That that
would be enough.'

'Why didn't you do that?'

'It wouldn't have done any good. Her heart – no, not her
heart, her mind, for she was crafty and knew what she was
doing – her mind was set, and she would not abandon her
hopes. I told her the box would have to go. "Does that mean
I am to go, too?" she said. "Yes," I said, for by now I could
see no other way. "It will hurt Karim," she said. "So be it," I
said. She bowed her head. But I could see she still hoped. So
I said: "It does not have to be like this." She looked at me
quickly. "Does it not?" she said. And I could see that she still
hoped. "Set your hopes lower," I said, "and you can still have
him."'

She stopped. When she continued, it was in a kind of mutter.
'I thought that perhaps we could come to some agreement.
That she could stay here, in the house, with him. But not as
his wife. I thought that perhaps his father would accept that.
And the family. Why should they not? They already knew
about Karim, about what kind of person he was. Every family,

even a Pasha's family, has secrets. Let them accept him, as he was. And if they could do that, perhaps they could accept the girl also. Every family has its handmaids and no one questions how far their service goes. Why should it not be like that with Karim and Soraya?'

'Did you put this to your husband?' asked Mahmoud.

'No. For Soraya wouldn't have it. She had seen me weaken, and she thought she had only to go on and I would give way. Completely. She was, in the end, like her father. Foolish, narrow, limited. I knew her mother. If she had been alive it would probably have been managed. But the mother was dead, and she would not listen to me.'

'So she had to go again,' said Mahmoud. 'And this time for good.'

'This time for good,' agreed the Pasha's lady.

'Was that what you told Suleiman?' asked Mahmoud.

The lady looked startled.

'Suleiman?' she said. 'Why should I tell Suleiman?'

'I just wondered if you had told Suleiman.'

'About the girl?' said the Pasha's lady, with a flash of anger. 'I did not *need* to tell Suleiman. He knew.'

'*What* did he know?'

'About the girl? All. Everything. He was with me when I came from the Sudan. He stayed with me when I moved out of my husband's house. He was with me when Soraya came. From the start he had said: "That girl is no good. She will do harm here before she is done." He is my eyes and ears. Know? Of course he knew! He had seen her from the start. "That girl has designs," he said. "She is not content to be a lowly servant." But I did not listen to him. I thought I knew best. Soraya spoke my tongue. I knew her mother. So I trusted her. I advanced her. And look how she repaid me!'

'You say that Suleiman knew all this?'

'From the start.'

'He knew about Karim?'

'Of course he knew about Karim! He had held him in his arms when he was small.'

'And when he grew. So he knew about Ibrahim?'

The Pasha's lady gave him a startled look. 'Yes,' she said,

'he knew about Ibrahim. He was here when it happened. But why do you ask? What has Ibrahim to do with all this?'

'I do not know,' said Mahmoud. 'That is why I am asking.'

'Ibrahim had nothing to do with any of this.'

'But Suleiman knew?'

'Of course. Why do you ask these questions?'

'Was Suleiman a kinsman of Ibrahim?'

'We are all kinspeople here.'

'In this house?'

'Yes.'

'But not your husband's house?'

'Both houses are my husband's.'

'But do both houses contain equally your kinspeople?'

'They do not. My kinspeople came with me to this house when my husband said I should go.'

'That Karim should go?'

'That Karim should go. Which is the same thing. I am his mother.'

'Let us go back,' said Mahmoud, 'to Soraya. And her bride box. When she left the second time, taking her bride box with her, who carried it for her?'

'Who carried it? I do not remember.'

'Men from your household?'

'I do not recall. No, I think not. They all wished to have done with Soraya.'

'So who were they?'

'I do not recall. These things are small.'

'When she came the second time, bringing her bride box, who brought it?'

'I do not recall.'

'I don't think it was people from your household.'

'No. It wasn't.'

'So who was it?'

'I do not recall.'

'It was the slaver's men.'

'Was it?'

'You had spoken with the slaver before. He had acted for you with Soraya's father. How was that?'

'I do not recall.'

'Not all people have dealings with slavers. How comes it that you did?'

'I knew Abdulla of old,' said the lady, sulkily. 'And I knew that he was passing so I asked him to act for me.'

'How did you know that he was passing?'

'Some of his people knew some of my people.'

'Because they come from the Sudan?'

'Yes. Because they come from the Sudan. From that part of the Sudan where my family lives.'

'What were the names of the men the slaver sent to collect the box?'

'I don't know. These are small things.'

'Someone must have instructed them. Was it Suleiman?'

'I don't recall.'

'It would have been, wouldn't it? Suleiman was your right-hand man. He acted for you in most things.'

'All this is too far distant—'

Mahmoud cut her short. 'What I want to know,' he said, 'is what instructions he gave to the slaver's men?'

'How do I know?'

'Suleiman would not have given instructions if he had not received instructions.'

He waited.

The lady said nothing.

'So what were they?'

The lady merely shrugged.

'I would have asked Suleiman,' said Mahmoud, 'but you had sent him away. So that I could not.'

After he had spoken to Karim, Owen went straight up to the temple.

The afternoon heat still hung over it. There was not a person about. Everyone had retreated indoors. Everything was silent. Only, high up on the pylon in front of the massive portico, he heard a slight buzzing and remembered the bees. He looked up, and in the different light he saw that they were not bees but wasps. He saw now that there were dozens of tiny wasps' nests, hanging from the stone like mud bubbles.

He stood there for a moment looking up at them. Then he heard the cry of a hawk, and stepped inside.

Selim emerged from behind a pillar.

'The guns have come,' said Owen. 'They will soon be here.'

'They are here already,' said Selim.

He took Owen inside and led him to the chamber he had shown him before. In the darkness it seemed to have changed its shape. Then Owen saw that the change was due to boxes that had been stacked there. He gently prised up a slat on one of the boxes and looked inside and saw the guns: new ones, like Karim's.

He hammered the slat back into place. It left behind it a slight smell of metal and grease.

'The men will be back,' Owen said. 'Probably soon.'

Selim nodded.

'I will be here,' he said.


Owen went round to the station office, where he found the clerk's brother, Babikr, standing in again. His brother, he said, was still sleeping it off after his exertion on the previous day.

'The boxes I spoke of—'

'Have arrived,' said Babikr. 'A man was sent to tell me. They are kept I know not where, but tomorrow they will be brought to the station just before the train arrives. There is a goods train, Effendi, early in the afternoon, and the boxes are to be put on it.'


'Suleiman had been sent away on a family matter,' said the Pasha's lady. 'Nothing to do with this or you.'

'We shall see what he says.'

'He is far away,' said the lady, 'and will not be coming back.'

'The Khedive's reach is long,' said Mahmoud.

'But does not extend to the Sudan,' said the lady.

'But the British are there as here,' said Mahmoud, 'and they will send him back for me to talk to him.'

The lady did not reply. In fact, she continued to sit there in silence, thinking. 'And all this,' she said after a while, 'for a silly girl!'

'For a girl, yes,' said Mahmoud, thinking that the lady was merely reflecting the general designation of women in the eyes of Arab society.

'And no one thinks of Karim,' said the lady.

'His mother thinks of him,' said Mahmoud. 'And that is right. But the girl had a mother, too, who, if she had been alive, would have been thinking of her.'

The Pasha's lady sat silent again for, it seemed, a long time. Mahmoud, however, was prepared to wait. 'Her mother is dead,' said the lady suddenly, 'so I had to do the thinking for her.'

'For the mother?'

'For her, yes. Since she is not alive and I am the senior kinswoman.'

'Was that why you took Soraya into your service?'

'Yes. Especially since I knew her mother, and her father is a sot. It is as if she were parentless. I had responsibilities.'

'So you took her in?'

'Yes, but it did not work out. She was stubborn, obstinate. She would not listen to me. It would have been better if she had.'

'You cannot control a person's feelings.'

'No, but you can guide them. And that is what a parent should do. And I would have done – I *did* do – since I was in place of her mother. But she would not listen to me.'

'Her eyes were looking in a direction where you felt they should not.'

'*Could* not! I had to think of my family. Or, at least, my husband's family. As well as hers. Even then I might have managed it if she had not been so obstinate. So proud! I had found her another man. That was right, that was what I should do! But she would not have it.'

'Well, there is heart in this . . .'

'Not if you're a penniless girl, there isn't! It would have been a good match. Better than she would ever have hoped for on her own. She should have been pleased. Delighted! But still she clung to her first thought and would not let it go.'

'Karim, you mean?'

'Yes! And he was out of the question. And it would not

have been right. Karim is . . . well, you know how Karim is.
He could not be a good husband to her! Nor to anyone! Oh,
she felt tender towards him, and sorry for him. But that is not
the same thing. From her point of view, as well as from his,
it had to be stopped. So I tried to turn her eyes in a different
direction.'

'You tried to arrange a marriage for her?'

'Yes! In the ordinary way. It is what her mother would
have done. And her father should have done. So I spoke to
someone, and he agreed. He was willing to take her. And . . .
and she would not even have had to leave the house. She could
have gone on living there – yes. Yes, she could have gone on
being kind to Karim. Of course, she couldn't have . . . But,
then, poor boy, I don't think it could have happened anyway.
Not on his side. There was no question of that. And her husband
would not have minded. Not her being kind to Karim. Since
there could be no question of more. He was willing for it to
be like that; he knew Karim. I spoke to him about it and
he was willing for it to be like that. It would have solved all
the problems. She would have been happy, he would have
been happy. Karim would have been happy. But she could not
let it be so! She wanted more. More than we could give.'

'Who was this man?'

'Suleiman.'

There was a shift in the pattern of activity in the midan. Men
were carrying the sacks of trocchee shells to the railway line
and laying them alongside the track, and camels were coming
in steady succession to the station to pick up the bales of gum
arabic. When they were loaded, they were led to the far side
of the midan, where camels and men were assembling. The
camels were made to lie down but the loads were not removed.
Owen realized that they were getting ready to leave.

He went to the station office, where he found Babikr standing
in again. He said that his brother had still not recovered from
his long ride to the Pasha's estate and back.

'But all is in order, Effendi,' he assured Owen.

'The loads are being readied for departure,' said Owen.

'Yes, Effendi,' said Babikr. 'There is a goods train coming

in and the trocchee shells will be put on it. And some of the gum arabic. The rest will go by camel to the coast.'

'And the boxes?'

Babikr hesitated. 'Not here yet,' he said.

At the last moment, a train of donkeys appeared with the boxes. The donkeys were lined up beside the tracks and their drivers stood by them. Other men joined them.

And then Owen saw him – the white man he had caught watching him earlier. He came up and stood by the boxes and appeared to be counting them. Apparently he was satisfied, for he nodded and stood back.

In the distance a train blew its whistle and, shortly afterwards, came into sight. It drew into the station and stopped. Immediately, there was a frenzy of activity. The doors of the wagons were thrown open and the sacks and bales put inside.

The boxes were loaded separately in a special wagon. The white man stood over the loading until it was complete and the door slammed closed again. Then he stepped away. He watched until the train drew out of the station.

'Clarke Effendi likes to see that all is done as he had decreed,' said Babikr.

'And was Suleiman content?' asked Mahmoud.

'He was content,' said the Pasha's lady. 'His other wife is growing old. And, besides, he knew he would be well rewarded.'

'But Soraya was not content?'

'No.'

'Did Suleiman know this?'

'He knew it and was angered. Who was Soraya, a poor basket maker's daughter, to set herself up against a Pasha's lady and a man of worth? Again, you see, it was presumption. "She will need to have it knocked out of her," he said, "and that I will do. I promise you, after we are married."'

'Did her father know about this?' asked Mahmoud.

'Mustapha?' The lady hesitated. 'He knew I had marriage in mind for her. But I had not mentioned Suleiman's name. It was not settled.'

'He still hoped, perhaps with her, that . . .'

'He was as foolish as his daughter. But the thing about a man like Mustapha is that, for the price of a drink, he will do whatever you ask. He was of no account.'

'But Suleiman was of account?'

'A worthy man,' said the Pasha's lady. 'Too worthy for a girl like her.'

'He knew what you were thinking of?'

'Of course.'

'And when he learned that she had refused him, was he angered?'

'Of course. What man would not be? A chit of a girl! Who thought herself too good to be a servant with the other servants!'

'And, of course, Suleiman was one of those servants.'

'The thought that she might look down on him was intolerable to him. As anyone would expect!'

'He was angered?'

'Who would not be?'

'And when he learned that she had refused him . . .?'

'Angered again. But, perhaps, knowing who she was, and what she was like, not discontent.'

'Yet angered,' said Mahmoud. 'And he was the one who was giving the slaver's men their instructions?'

The Pasha's lady said nothing.

'Again I ask,' said Mahmoud, 'what were those instructions?'

'And again I reply,' said the Pasha's lady, 'that I do not know.'

'But you must know. For you first gave Suleiman the instructions.'

'I instructed him to tell them that they were to take her home, and her accursed bride box with her.'

'And that was all?'

The lady was silent again. Then she gave a little shiver. 'I know what you are thinking. But that was all.'

As Mahmoud rode back to Denderah, he was not displeased with the way things had gone. He felt that his investigation had advanced. True, there were further questions to be asked. But he felt that the number of people of whom they had to be asked had narrowed down. Admittedly, it was not going to be easy to ask them, since Suleiman was in the Sudan and

likely to remain there: and the slavers were who knew where.
But Suleiman would in the end be reached, and so, he thought,
would be the slavers. They might well be in the same place.
Their actual apprehension might have to be left to others.
But in the end they would be brought home to the Parquet
roost.

There was, he thought, little more that he could do here. So
he was not as depressed, or as angered, as he might have been
when he got back to Denderah and found a message recalling
him at once to Cairo. Not as angered as he might have been,
but nevertheless very surprised.

# TEN

O wen was surprised, too, and thoughtful. Was this an expression of rivalries inside the Parquet? Of the jealousies of the old? He knew that Mahmoud's speedy ascent was resented by some inside the Parquet. Mahmoud had told him that some of the senior people there had it in for him because of his political sympathies, that possibly his very assignment to the case had been a means of getting him out of the way. Owen thought that sometimes Mahmoud's fear was overdone but guessed there might be something in it.

But what troubled him was the possibility that Mahmoud had been whisked back to Cairo precisely because someone there was worried that he was actually getting somewhere. And didn't want him to.

And how far was this connected with the slavery issue? Strictly speaking, that was Owen's concern and not Mahmoud's; but the two cases – Soraya's murder and the revival of slaving – were connected, and perhaps others knew that as well as he did. It was something to be looked into when he returned to Cairo.

And, fortunately, that was just about to happen. The action had moved on, almost certainly into the Sudan, and there was little point in him staying on here. Apart from anything else, by this time the mountains of papers on his desk would be toppling over and something had to be done about them. Nikos, who, he knew, believed that any time spent out of the office was time ill-spent, wanted him back.

There were one or two things, however, to be settled before he left. The first was what was to be done about Mustapha. Clearly he had to be formally charged and brought before a court. Owen himself could not do this: all that sort of thing had to be handed over to the Parquet. In fact, formally, it had already been handed over to the Parquet, in the shape of Mahmoud.

He and Mahmoud discussed the matter. Mahmoud agreed to bring Mustapha before a court. The question, though, was which court. The obvious answer was the one in Cairo. But there were arguments against that. In Cairo the trial could easily become enmeshed in politics and not get anywhere. Denderah was a long way from Cairo. Especially in terms of the urgency with which the legal system would address it. Better somewhere away from Cairo, sophisticated enough to be able to handle the issue, not so sophisticated as to be more interested in playing political games than bringing the issue to a conclusion. They decided that Mahmoud would take him to Luxor. The court there was sufficiently developed to be able to take on the trial and, being closer to the scene of the crime, might even be able to address it more easily.

So Mahmoud and Mustapha took the train south and Owen the next train north. Owen was the only passenger to get on at Denderah. He looked for Clarke but did not see him. Bibikr, who had come to the station to see Owen off, said he would have gone back to the coast with the gum arabic.

Owen was a little surprised at this, given Clarke's previous fussiness over the guns and his insistence on overseeing personally anything to do with guns. No doubt, though, he would have made special arrangements.

Owen, of course, had also made arrangements.

'I don't know that I can!' said Nassir, the warehouse clerk. 'I'm that busy this morning!'

'Too busy for a cup of coffee?' said Georgiades, affecting amazement.

'Well . . .'

'Not even one?'

'A quick one!' stipulated the clerk.

Which stretched until it was no longer a quick one – but, then, there was a lot to catch up on after the weekend and the latest reckless ventures of Georgiades' wife.

'But hasn't she got shopping to do?'

'Tell me about it!' said the Greek gloomily.

'A man must eat!'

'Oh, I eat all right. She looks after that side well.'

'But not the other side?' said Nassir hopefully. The Greek was sparing of details but the clerk had gathered the impression that that side was pretty good, too; remarkably so, in fact.

'Take aubergines,' said the Greek.

'Aubergines?' said Nassir, disappointed.

'She went down to the market this morning to get some. A few, for lunch. And she came back with two barrow loads! "What's this?" I said. "Are we feasting the neighbourhood, or something?"

'"That's an idea!" she said. "We could charge twenty *piastres* a head. Two hundred and fifty people – I could get more aubergines if I haven't got enough. That's five thousand piastres. Cost, definitely less than two. That's three thousand profit. With that I could buy . . ."

'"Just stick to aubergines," I said. "And my lunch!" But there you are, you see: she goes out to buy a simple thing and finishes by buying up the whole market!'

'May Allah preserve us!' said Nassir. 'She goes out to buy a few things for your lunch, and in a moment she's disrupted the whole economy! There's suddenly a shortage of aubergines!'

'And the trouble about *that*,' said the Greek, 'is that it pushes the price of aubergines up, and then she comes back to the market and makes a killing! And everybody else in the market is going mad!'

'The worries of having a wife!'

The clerk looked reluctantly at his watch. 'I have to go. There is much to do today, with Clarke Effendi coming back.'

'He's coming back, is he?'

'Sent a message.'

'And what about the goods?'

'They'll be arriving on the train before. I've got to get down there and see them off the train. He doesn't like to have them hanging about by themselves even for a moment.'

'And then you've got to move them on, I suppose.'

'First, to the warehouse, and then on from there afterwards. But he likes to see to that himself.'

'Another night job.'

'It could be. It very well could.'

'You'd best be getting along, then. And I've got to be getting back to my wife. To stop her.'

'Stop her?'

'She's thinking of putting the money she makes from the aubergines into night dresses.'

'Night dresses!' said Nassir, sitting down again.

'She knows a chap who's got a lot of night dresses on his hands. A shop went bust and left him with a lot of stock to dispose of. She reckons she could get them for two piastres each. Now, four hundred and sixty at two piastres . . .'

But, enticing as this prospect was, from more than one point of view, the warehouse clerk was forced to tear himself away.

The Greek ambled along the street, exchanging greetings with everyone he passed, calling in at the barber's for a brief word which became several words, and coming to a stop at the broad pan of the pavement restaurant, where he sniffed the air appreciatively.

'It's different,' he said.

'Always the same!' decreed the restaurant owner. 'We never change.'

'Is it the oil?'

'Just the same. It may be slightly different this morning,' he conceded. 'We've opened a new tin. But the oil is just the same. I get it from Feisal.'

He dipped a spoon in and tasted it. 'Well, *I* think it's just the same!' he said. 'Here, you try.'

The Greek sipped. 'I can't taste any difference,' he admitted. 'It was just that, coming down the street this morning, it struck me as different.'

'You're tasting the newness. The oil is just the same but it's fresh from the can.'

'That must be it.'

The Greek squatted down beside the pan.

'Of course, it's a bit early for lunch . . .'

'Oh, come on – try a bit!'

'Well, just one. A little kebab.'

The restaurant owner watched him.

'Delicious!' the Greek said appreciatively.

The owner, relaxing, went back to his chopping of vegetables.

'Hello!' the Greek said, catching sight of his neighbour. 'It's Abdul, isn't it? Nothing on this morning?'

'Just carried a wardrobe.'

'Then you'll need something to restore you!'

He signalled to the owner, who dipped some beans into the bowl before Abdul.

'I haven't forgotten you,' said the Greek. 'I've got something coming along. It'll be a rush job.'

'How rush?'

'The next couple of days. It's on its way. A handy load.'

'If it's too big, I can't do it. I've got something on.'

'I expect you could fit this one in. It comes in bits. You could do part of it tomorrow, part the next day, and then fit it in. The thing about it is that my friend pays well – over the odds. But it's got to be fitted in, like I said.'

'When would I know?'

'Soon. It's worth putting yourself out for. As I say, he pays over the odds. It's delicate, you see.'

'Perishable?'

'Fragile, rather. You'd have to be very careful with it. That's why he doesn't want just anybody. He's got to be strong, but careful with it.'

'Experienced!' said the porter.

'As my wife says, a bit of experience goes a long way!'

'She says that, does she?' said the porter, grinning.

'Tells in my favour,' said the Greek. 'And at my age you need something that tells in your favour!'

'You need size, too. And energy!'

'I had the size. But now I've lost the energy.'

'Pity!'

'It matters. You see, my wife is younger than I am.'

'That has its advantages.'

'True. But sometimes I worry . . . The thing is, she's a bit of a beauty. Was a dancing girl.'

'A dancing girl?'

'Yes. Very supple. You'd be surprised!'

'She can get up to things, can she?'

'Oh, yes. She's a bit older now than when we first married, but she's still . . . well, you know!'

'Oh, yes, I know!'

'She's still got her figure. A regular Scheherazade!'

'But misses the energy?'

'I'm afraid so.'

'Well, that's not all bad, is it?'

'No, but it's demanding.'

'You can't keep up?'

'Not any more. You'd need to be, well, like the Khedive himself. If half of what I've heard is true.'

'It's having so many wives that does it. Keeps you in trim.'

'One's enough for me!'

'Especially if she's the way you say she is!'

'The trouble is, I'm out so much.'

'That must be a real worry. In the circumstances.'

'Oh, it is. You see, I can't keep my eye on her all the time. I've got a job to do, after all.'

'Well, yes. Look, I'm around quite a bit of the time. I'll keep a lookout and tip you the word if I see anything going on.'

'Would you?'

'No problem at all!' said Abdul, grinning.

Abdul was still sitting at the pavement restaurant the next time the Greek went past. He dropped down beside him.

'The work's not come through yet, then?'

'No. The stuff is coming in by train and it's not here yet. But Nassir likes me to be right at hand when it does. His boss likes it to be just so. And if it's not, he kicks Nassir's backside! When it's coming up, Nassir gets all edgy.'

'It's for Nassir, is it? He was telling me about it. He's got to be here himself, he was saying, and right on the dot!'

'That's right. And he wants me to stay close while it's on the boil. That's why I'm sitting around here. The moment the train gets in I've got to get everyone together so that we can go over the moment he gives us the say-so. We've not to be on the platform; his boss doesn't like that. He says it draws attention to the consignment. So we've got to be just round the corner and then get round there in a flash. And then it's pick the boxes up – and they're bloody heavy, too – and take them round to the warehouse immediately, with Nassir leading the way and his boss right behind us breathing down our necks!'

'Gets you a bit edgy, too, I would think!' said the Greek sympathetically.

'Oh, I don't mind it,' said Abdul. 'The money's good, and it doesn't last long. And then we're off round to the beerhouse the moment after.'

'That's all right, then,' said the Greek, laughing.

'I'm not saying that it's not. Mind you, as I say to Nassir, it's not the smartest way of doing things. Because we've got to move them on again afterwards, and if we did it at the same time and just moved them on straightaway to where they've got to go, it would save time and money. But I'm not really complaining. That way he does it makes two jobs out of one, so that's better for us.'

'Is the second move a big one? Much of a carry?'

'No. It's just around the corner, to the *madrassa*. It doesn't take a moment and it would be easy for us to do the first time.'

'You don't want to tell him that,' said the Greek.

'I don't reckon Nassir wants to tell him that,' said Abdul. 'Otherwise it would all have been done in the one job years ago. But I reckon that this way Nassir makes something out of it.'

'That's the way of the world!' said the Greek.

Although he gave no outward sign of it, the moment the porter mentioned the madrassa, Georgiades become alert. Madrassas were schools. Not the new state schools the government was building, but the old, traditional, religious schools. They came in various shapes and sizes. Usually they took the form of pupils gathered around a teacher who would instruct them in the Koran. Instruction meant learning by heart. The leader would read or recite a passage from the Koran and the pupils would repeat it until they were word perfect. There was some explanation of the passage but the main thing was to commit it to heart.

Often the teaching would take place not in the classroom but beneath pillars of a mosque. The teacher would sit with his back against one of the pillars and the pupils would gather round him. Sometimes the pupils were very young, barely more than toddlers, not even carrying slates. But sometimes they were burly adolescents who used their slates not for writing on but as missiles. You would find them setting the pace in almost any riot.

Usually the rioting was spontaneous, a bit of adolescent fun, on the whole harmless, as Owen had to frequently point out to his superiors, both Khedivial and British. But sometimes it was not and then, often, it was not fun. The madrassas frequently served as centres for radical movements drawing on the young. Cairo abounded in political societies and many of these were based on or grew out of madrassas.

Madrassas were the bane of Nikos's life. They were always causing trouble. He monitored them as best he could; he had a list of them as long as your arm. But they kept coming and going; they were essentially fluid and difficult to keep track of. Some were religious in orientation and some were exclusively political; some were reformist and many revolutionary. Some were violent.

If trouble was coming, it was usually coming from the madrassas.

So when Georgiades reported back to Nikos what the porter had said, Nikos immediately switched on. He knew from long experience that this was the moment when you could nip potential violence in the bud. It wasn't a long moment; it could burst into open rioting very quickly, and then it was very difficult to deal with. But, just for a moment, if you could intervene early and decisively, you could stop it in its tracks.

The important thing was early intelligence, which, he thought, in this case he had acquired. But he had not yet got enough. He sent Georgiades out again. This was their job: to find out what they could. And then present their findings to the Mamur Zapt, who would decide on the necessary action. That was not his concern, for which Nikos thanked God. He knew he wouldn't be good at it. Fortunately, Owen was returning. And not, Nikos told himself and everyone, before time.

Georgiades had taken up position in the goods part of the Pont Limoun. From where he was standing, at the very edge of the area, just where it gave on to the main station with its bustling passengers, he could see Nassir waiting nervously. From time to time he walked off agitatedly but he always returned to the spot he had chosen.

The goods train from Luxor pulled in. Immediately there was a great banging of doors and cries from the porters. Goods were brought down from the wagons on to the platform and porters began taking them away. Nassir, however, did not move.

He did not move until the bustle had subsided and most of the goods which had been unloaded had been either taken away or stacked on the platform. Then, when everything was quieter, Nassir moved forward.

The wagon before which he had stationed himself had not so far been opened. Now a man came up and began to unlock it. The door was pulled open and the station porters started to unload. They put the loads, heavy wooden boxes, carefully on the platform. Nassir was standing within a yard of them, so close as almost to get in the porter's way. When they had finished, he counted the boxes. Then he stuck his head into the wagon to make sure that none had been left behind.

Satisfied on that score he went back to the boxes already piled there. Then he stood there keeping an eye on them while the station porters moved on to their next task.

He stood there for nearly an hour and then Clarke Effendi appeared, coming from the passenger area. He walked straight over to the boxes and began counting them, hardly sparing a word for Nassir, who hovered beside him. When he had finished counting, he said something to Nassir and Nassir signalled to someone at the end of the goods platform. In a moment, Abdul appeared with a crowd of burly porters. They began to pick up the boxes. The boxes were heavy and even Abdul could not manage one by himself.

With two men to a box, there were a lot of porters, and Georgiades saw that there had been a lot of work behind the scenes. By Nassir, presumably. Now they were here, though, it did not take long. They formed up in a convoy, with Nassir leading the way and Clarke coming behind. Once or twice he snapped something at a porter who had fallen short.

The convoy was moving out of the station, with Georgiades not far behind, when suddenly he saw Zeinab and Leila. They were crossing the Place Bab el Hadid, just in front of the Douane, the big Customs Office, when Clarke saw them.

He ran to the front of the convoy and seized Nassir by the arm. 'That girl!' he said, pointing to Leila. 'Who is she?'

'I don't know!' said Nassir, clearly taken aback.

'Find out!'

Nassir hesitated, and said something. Probably he was asking what Clarke wanted him to do: stay with the convoy, or follow Zeinab and Leila? It was obviously the latter, for Nassir detached himself from the porters and went away after Zeinab and Leila.

Georgiades wondered what to do. Ought he to follow Zeinab and Leila in case of trouble? Trouble? From Nassir? He didn't think that likely. Besides, he could find out from Nassir later what had happened. And Zeinab and Leila, of course.

No, the thing to do was stick with the convoy. They would surely be going to Nassir's warehouse. But guns were guns, and Georgiades knew that the one thing he must not do was lose sight of them. If by some chance they did not go to the warehouse, and were lost in the warren of Cairo's back streets, Owen would never forgive him.

Zeinab had picked up Leila from the kindergarten that morning. She often did so these days. They would usually go to the Hotel Continentale for an ice cream, which you could have sitting out on the terrace. Leila liked that because while you sat there you could watch the tumblers turning cartwheels along the street in front of you and the street sellers parading up and down with their monkeys. Sometimes the street sellers would poke their wares through the balustrade at the tourists. The tourists at the Continentale were European or American but not English, which suited Zeinab. The English usually went to Shepheard's.

After they had had their ice creams they would walk home for lunch. By this time, after the morning at school, Leila would be getting tired. If it was Musa, not Zeinab, who was with her, he would usually pick her up at this point and carry her but Zeinab just held her hand. When they got home they would have lunch in the cool of the kitchen – there would be no cooking in the kitchen until Musa's wife was preparing the evening meal. By that time Leila would just be getting up, as she went to bed after lunch for an hour or so.

Zeinab increasingly liked these moments together with Leila. They brought a bit of peace into her life, too; and whereas at one time she had enjoyed her morning gossips with her friends in their homes or the big European style – indeed, Parisian style – shops, now she liked the artless chats about the morning's school that she had with Leila and with Leila's friend, Aisha's daughter.

Like Aisha, too, she was missing her other half. Owen had not been away for very long but she was used to having him around, and with him away everything felt slightly odd. Which was, perhaps, another reason for her turning increasingly towards Leila. She wondered what it would be like when Owen got back. She hadn't really seen much of him with children and wondered how he would get on. When she had seen him with children they had seemed to get along very well, but having a child constantly in the house was different.

And would Leila be constantly in the house when Owen got back? This, he had told her, was a temporary arrangement, a means of safeguarding the child until they had got the slavers behind bars. When they had – and Zeinab was quite confident that Owen would do that – what then?

Mahmoud had got in that evening, tired after the journey and a little subdued. Aisha couldn't make out whether things had gone well or whether they hadn't. She knew he was angered and depressed at being so cavalierly, as he felt, summoned back to Cairo before he had quite finished the case. Why had he been? Aisha feared that he had crossed some political bigwig with influence in the Parquet. This had happened before, and was always likely to happen, with Mahmoud so fierce about his political commitments. Aisha was with Mahmoud every inch of the way on these, but sometimes she wished that his career progression was a smoother one.

He seemed a little downcast, which, again, was not unusual with him at the end of a case. No matter how successful he had been, somehow it always fell short of what he had hoped. This was usually part of a passing phase and she hoped it was the same this time.

A lot, apparently, turned on this man Suleiman. But he, it seemed, was now in the Sudan, where Mahmoud could not reach him. Mahmoud, in fact, was not too despondent about this. He knew that if he could not reach him, Owen probably could. There were advantages sometimes, thought Aisha darkly, in the English having power all over the place. Mahmoud had told her about this poor girl. It had put Aisha in an untypical fury. To treat a young girl like that! It was typical of the way women were treated in Egypt. And she was proud, very proud, that it was her husband who was leading the battle against it.

Mahmoud was glad to be home. It was frustrating to be dragged away just when he felt he was getting somewhere. But it wasn't the end. Either he would still get somewhere or, if they had put someone else on the case, then that someone else would. Soraya would not go unavenged. It might take time – more time than he had thought – if, as now appeared, the politicians were taking a hand in it. If they were, there would be a struggle in the Parquet. But there were enough young men in the Parquet these days for the battle not to be hopeless. And he himself would take a hand in it. Now that he was back in Cairo he could play an active part in any politicking. They would see!

But, meanwhile, he was feeling a little puzzled. Just before he had got on the train a man had dashed up to him. He had been sent, he said, by the Pasha's lady. And he was to tell Mahmoud that the Pasha's lady had been summoned to Cairo, too. By her husband. And would shortly be arriving.

This was an unexpected turn of events. He had thought that the Pasha and his wife were so utterly at loggerheads that there could be no prospect of them coming together; much less of the Pasha actually inviting – or perhaps it was summoning – her. Or of her agreeing to come if he did.

And why was she telling him – and going out of her way to tell him?

The thought came to him that perhaps she wanted someone to know. In case she didn't come back.

# ELEVEN

'Well,' said the genial Greek, as he stuck his head in at the warehouse the next morning. 'So it's all safely stowed, is it?'

'It is,' said Nassir, 'and I can breathe again!'

'And have a cup of coffee?'

'I don't know that I should,' wavered Nassir. 'He might come in early to have a look around.'

'He was in last night, wasn't he?'

'He was. I don't mind that. He wanted to make sure everything was all right. Well, that's his way. But he should have gone away afterwards. Some of us have lives to live, you know.'

'Is that what you told him?' said the Greek admiringly.

'Well . . .' said the clerk, tempted. 'No,' he admitted. 'Not exactly.'

'More than your job's worth?'

'Exactly!'

'But once it was all settled, you'd have thought . . .'

'You would. You would have thought he'd have gone home, instead of fussing around. But he didn't. He had to go over it all again, making sure everything was as it should be. Not just the lot that had just come in, but everything else! Fussing around. And what made it worse was that he had sent me off.'

'Sent you off?'

'Yes. Before we'd even got back to the warehouse. Just like that: on a whim. He'd seen some kid or other out with her mother and wanted me to follow her and find out where she lived! Now, if it had been the mother, I'd have understood. She was a real looker. But a kid! I mean . . .!'

'He's not . . .' said the Greek, hesitating. 'One of those?'

'Not as far as I know. As I say, I'd have thought the mother was more in his line. But you can never tell with him. He's full of quirks. Whims. I don't know what it was all about but he had me follow them. And then when I got back, he wanted to know all about it. Where they had gone, that sort of thing. Well, they'd gone to have an ice cream, like any sensible mother would when she'd got her kid hanging about her on a hot afternoon.'

'Did you tell him that?'

'Well . . .'

'You should have. Probably not got any kids himself so wouldn't know.'

'That could well be true.'

'Not got any family of his own?'

'I wouldn't think so. Going off on those long journeys of his all the time. What woman would stand it?'

'Maybe that's why he wanted to know? To find out what ordinary life was like?'

'Seems a funny thing to do to me. But that's what he did. Sent me off after them. And, you know, he'd made such a fuss earlier about the consignment and the way it was handled. Me at the front, him at the back. And then he sends me away after some kid!'

'A nutter!' judged the Greek. 'They're all like that, these bosses.'

'Well, this one is a prize specimen.'

'Look, how about that coffee? I can see this must all have been a strain for you.'

'So now you've got it all in,' said the Greek over coffee, 'is that it for a while?'

'No. It's got to go out again. In a few days' time.'

'Have I got it wrong, or did you say it had to go to a madrassa?'

'You've not got it wrong. The one round the corner.'

'Round the corner? Why didn't they take it there in the first place, then?'

'Safer in the warehouse, I suppose. You don't want it hanging around in the madrassa. They've only got the one room in the mosque.'

'And the kids, I suppose. They'd have it to bits in a moment.'

'Don't say things like that! My hair's grey enough as it is.'

'Well, once it gets there, it's out of your hands, anyway.'

'That's right. And not a moment too soon.'

The clerk couldn't stay long. There was always the chance that Clarke Effendi would come round.

'Keeps you up to the mark, I can see.'

'It's only for a short time. Then he goes away again.'

'He doesn't fuss around at the madrassa?'

'Once it gets there, it's not his concern.'

'Moves on, I suppose. Quite quickly. You say they've not got much room there.'

'That's right.'

'Why bring it here, then? I take it that it's for other places as well as the madrassa. Other madrassas, I suppose. Tables and chairs, that sort of thing.'

'They could certainly do with some. Although I'm not sure it's that. Clarke Effendi doesn't always tell me.'

'I'll tell you what I think it is,' said the Greek. 'It'll be part of all the money the government is spending on schools. Too much, in my view.'

'And in mine . . .'

Georgiades, sweating in the heat, padded patiently round the corner to the madrassa the clerk had mentioned. It was in a mosque, as Nassir had said. Not strictly in it, but on the steps in front of it, where other people, too, besides the teacher and his pupils, had gathered beneath the pillars in the shade. The pupils at the moment were young children, gripping their slates tightly. From time to time the teacher would pause in his recitation and get them to write a text, usually a verse from the Koran. They would hold up their slates to show him and he would check to see that they had got it right. For it wasn't simply a matter of getting the letters and spelling correct, it was also doing justice to the Holy Word.

Behind them, on the outskirts of the group, were older boys not involved for the moment but waiting more or less patiently for their turn. And behind them, also sitting on the steps, were a lot of casual onlookers, talking quietly among themselves but benefiting, too, from hearing the Holy Words.

'Good words!' said the Greek, sitting down with his back to a pillar and mopping his face.

One or two of the people around him nodded. He tried to draw them into conversation but found their talk hard to follow. They weren't very forthcoming, either, so after a while he abandoned the attempt. Sitting there with his back to the pillar in the heat, among the gentle hum of the teacher's words, and the conversation around about him, he dozed off.

When he awoke he heard people talking. They were different people from the ones he had been sitting by before; they were more talkative. They were talking about beds, a congenial topic for Georgiades just at the moment.

They came from outside Cairo. You could hear it in their voices. But he wasn't at once able to place them. Then he caught the work '*angareeb*'. An angareeb was a sort of rope bed, more common in the south of Egypt than in the city, but not unusual among the less well-to-do. There were no springs, no bottom layer, just rope, interwoven to form a comfortable, slatted surface, without even the give of a hammock.

Now they were talking about *andats*. He knew vaguely what they were, although again the word was unfamiliar. A foreign term for a foreign thing. You didn't find them in Egypt. Thank goodness, for they appeared to be a species of stink bug: a sort of winged louse, from what he could make out. If you trod on one it gave off a most abominable smell. Sometimes they fell into the soup.

Soup? Had he misheard? No, they were talking about a child who had swallowed one by mistake. They had to call a *hakim*, a doctor.

Georgiades didn't like the sound of this and was glad when they turned to another topic. It was, however, another medical matter. One of the speakers apparently had marital difficulties. He blamed his wife. She blamed him. Whoever was to blame, the problem appeared to be that appetite was inadequate.

'Why don't you try trocchee shells?' someone suggested.

*Trocchee shells?* Georgiades came suddenly awake.

'What do you do?' said the afflicted man doubtfully. 'Swallow them?'

'No, no, not just like that. First you grind them into powder. The Saudis are always doing it.'

'Trocchee shells? I don't think that sounds very nice. Not to eat, I mean. Hey, wait a minute! That's another thing with a nasty smell, isn't it? Are you having me on?'

'No! No, apparently it works a treat. In Saudi they're all trying it.'

'Dirty bastards!'

'I know someone . . . five times a night!'

'How do you get hold of it?'

'There's a chap round the corner . . . His boss is big in it . . . Trocchee shells, I mean. That's what he trades in. You make them into buttons.'

'Trocchee shells?'

'That's right.'

'But how do you . . .?

'No, no, normally they just get made into buttons. But in Saudi Arabia, apparently, they grind them into powder, and then away you go!'

And now Georgiades got it. *Angareeb*, *andat*, trocchee shells, the way they spoke . . . The people here were all Sudanese.

Mahmoud was to be put on to another case. 'Why?' he asked.

'Mercy,' said his boss. 'Why should you fry in the sticks when there's work to be done here?'

'I don't like to leave it unfinished . . .'

'You're not. According to what you say in your report, you've about finished it already. It's just waiting for us to pick up this bloke Suleiman, and our friends in the Sudan will do that for us. They'll send him here and he'll sing sweetly and after that it's only a matter of picking up some hooligans in . . . what was the name of the place, if it has a name? Denderah. And any fool can do it. We'll send someone down. We might even get the police to do it. They cock up most things but they ought to be able to manage a simple arrest. It's just manhandling. You've done all the brain work.'

'Yes, but . . .' said Mahmoud weakly. 'It's not *quite* wrapped up yet . . .'

'It will be,' said his boss confidently. 'When you get this bloke Suleiman here.'

'It will be me that gets to question him, will it?' asked Mahmoud.

'I expect so,' said his boss vaguely. 'Anyway, it will be brought to court, so you'd better start pulling things together. Wasn't there a bride box in it somewhere?'

The bride box had all this time been resting quietly in the yard at the Bab-el-Khalk, the police headquarters where Owen had his office. It had been left sufficiently far away from the main building for the smell to be manageable and it had become less unpleasant with the passage of time. At first, people had wondered what it was doing there but as the days passed they ceased to wonder and took it so much for granted that they hardly saw it. If anyone raised a question they were given the answer: 'The Mamur Zapt has decreed it,' which stopped argument.

One day Zeinab had to go in to the Bab-el-Khalk on an errand for her father. It was a trivial errand, a misplaced form or something, to do with her father's taxes. Nuri Pasha tried to avoid having anything directly to do with the tax authorities, and usually sent any tax return via Owen in the hope – misguided, of course, as most of Nuri's financial dealings were – that it would impress or even cow the Egyptian Finance Ministry. Owen always sent it on immediately without comment. Nothing good ever resulted from Nuri's tactics but he clung to them in hope. What, after all, was an eminent son-in-law (or might-be son-in-law) for? Believing that Owen was still away in the south, he decided on this occasion to make use of his daughter's service instead.

Zeinab, who, although cavalier with finances, especially her own, knew something about the way the system worked under the British, warned him that nothing would come of it and that he would do far better to get a good accountant. But Nuri shrank from accountants, particularly ones who knew what they were doing and who might discover what he had been doing, and persuaded her to keep to the usual time-honoured ways of Egypt. He even put a wad of notes in her hand, which she gratefully accepted but knew better than to use for the purpose he intended. Nuri Pasha was also a great believer in the personal touch, especially when it was delivered by a pretty girl. And what were daughters for, etc . . .?

Zeinab had nothing better to do that afternoon so agreed to go to the Bab-el-Khalk, stipulating, however, that all she would do would be to deliver the letter. 'Drop it on a desk.' Nuri Pasha had sufficient confidence in his daughter to believe that even dropping a letter on a desk would have an impact if it was done by her.

She took Leila with her. She had got into the way of taking her on brief expeditions and quite liked the experience of walking along hand-in-hand with the little girl.

When they entered the yard at the Bab-el-Khalk Leila saw the bride box and at once burst into tears. She broke away from Zeinab and rushed over to it.

'It's Soraya's box!' she cried. 'And it's all dusty. They haven't been looking after it properly!'

One or two orderlies standing nearby moved hastily away at this point. Nikos looked out of a window and then quietly closed the shutters.

McPhee, the eccentric but tender-hearted Deputy Commissioner, came out of his office and gave her a square of Turkish delight. 'It's all right, it's all right!' he said, distressed. 'It will clean up!'

'But it ought never to have been allowed to get like this!' cried Leila.

'It's evidence, you see, and evidence shouldn't be tampered with,' said McPhee.

'It's *not* evidence. It's Soraya's box!'

'I suppose it would do no harm if it was dusted . . .' said McPhee weakly. He looked around. 'Ya Hussein!' he called to an orderly sitting in the shade.

'Effendi,' said Hussein, springing up smartly.

'Dust the box!'

'Dust the . . .? began Hussein incredulously.

'It's dirty.'

'Well . . .'

Hussein pulled himself together. 'Ya Ali!' he called.

'Ya Hussein?'

Ali was, of course, the other half of the Hussein/Ali act. He came running – well, walking – round the corner.

'Dust the box!' said Hussein.

'Dust the . . .?'

'I will do it!' said Leila.

'Now, wait a minute, this is man's work. You can't just take a man's work away. Not like that. What am I going to live on? What about my family. My wife? My children?'

'Just bloody do it!' said McPhee.

'*I* will do it!' said Leila. 'Can I have a duster?'

'Ali . . .'

'Oh, all right,' said Ali, going back into the building. He emerged with a soft chamois leather, bright yellow duster.

Then he saw the box. 'It's that bride box again!' he said, taken aback.

'Soraya's,' said Leila.

'Yes, well . . .'

'It's all dirty.'

'Yes, well . . .'

'Give it to me and I'll do it!' said Leila, taking the duster.

'Now, now, wait a minute!'

'This is man's work!'

'Do it then!' snapped Zeinab.

'Dusting a bride box? Look, lady . . .'

'It's not any old bride box; it's Soraya's bride box!' said Leila.

'Why, it's that little girl again!' said Ali.

'I remember you!' said Leila. 'You were the nice man who . . .'

'I suppose we could help a bit,' said Hussein soft-heartedly.

'Dusting a bride box, though! I never thought it would come to this. I mean . . .'

'I wouldn't mind, but everybody's watching . . .'

Heads were popping out of every window. Including Nikos's.

'Everyone get back to work!' shouted McPhee.

'What the hell's going on?' shouted a new voice. It was Garvin, the Commandant of Police.

'Nothing, sir. Everything in control!' said McPhee swiftly.

Hussein seized back the duster and he and Ali began dusting furiously.

'Haven't you men got anything better to do?' demanded Garvin, coming out into the yard.

'I'm afraid, Commandant, it's my fault,' said Zeinab, stepping forward.

'Why, Zeinab, how nice to see you! But what are you doing here? Come inside.'

'Must be a Pasha's daughter at least,' muttered Hussein.

'The one they were sending that dog to, I'll bet!'

'Dog!' said Leila, beginning to cry again. 'In my sister's bride box!'

'Never mind, my little one!' said Hussein, who had daughters of his own and only occasionally felt like selling them into slavery. 'It's not there now, and we'll polish the box up so that it will look like new!'

When Zeinab and Leila got back to the house, Owen had returned from Denderah. Leila was suddenly shy at this stranger, although she remembered him as the funny man who had pulled faces at her. She hid behind Musa's wife in the kitchen and was only gradually coaxed out. Zeinab hadn't realized that there had been a weight on her shoulders but was now conscious that it had gone. Owen was pleased to be back with Zeinab and in a comfortable house again. He had grown used to and liked Arab houses, but they had their disadvantages and he missed English armchairs. Besides, he had not really been in a proper house since he left Cairo. It was good to be back.

It felt less good the next morning when he got into his office and saw the mountains of paperwork awaiting him. Nikos, he was convinced, had been building them up deliberately.

He looked first at the Brotherhood but all was as it had been. When he realized the scale of the arms shipments he had wondered if they were something to do with it, but on reflection it did not seem so. This was a new lot, which in a way was more worrying.

Nikos brought him up to date and then he had Georgiades in to give a report. All seemed satisfactory there, although he

knew that it was now top of his agenda. The slavery issue was
still there but had slipped down the agenda. The bride box
was even further down. But something to do with it was
niggling at the back of his mind and sooner or later he would
have to give it his attention.

Meanwhile, there was the paperwork. And what was this?
A missive from Nuri Pasha? One of those. He sent it on
automatically and without additional comment to the tax
people.

Towards the end of the afternoon he pushed all the papers
aside and sat there for some time thinking.

The next day was Friday, the Muslim sabbath, and all the
government offices were closed. Many of the officials who
worked in them were Copts, like Nikos, which meant that they
were Christian. Nevertheless, they took the Muslim sabbath.
And also the Christian Sunday, although there was argument
about this. As it happened, Nikos didn't usually bother about
sabbaths, either Muslim or Christian, and he was in early the
next morning when Owen arrived. Well, that was satisfying.
It meant that Owen's day was spoiled, which would teach him
not to go gallivanting off from the office when there was work
to do.

Through the window he could hear the *muezzin* giving the
morning call from the minaret, summoning the faithful to
prayers. To his surprise Owen got up and left, putting his
flowerpot-like red fez on his head.

He took a train the short distance across the city, getting
out not far from Nassir's warehouse. Then he walked round
the corner to the mosque Georgiades had told him about.
Already the faithful were streaming in.

The mosque was not one of Cairo's larger ones. It consisted
of porticoes surrounding a square court, in the centre of which
was a tank from which worshippers could scoop up water for
the necessary ablutions. Owen went across to it and washed
his hands three times and then splashed water on his face and
head, lifting up the fez to do so. Then he joined the rows of
worshippers before the Mecca-facing wall, took off his shoes
and placed them sole to sole on the matting before him at the

point where his head would touch the ground, and sat back on his haunches.

In front of him, on the exterior facing wall, was the *mihrab*, the niche which marked the direction of Mecca. To the right of this was the *mimbar*, or pulpit, and just in front of it was the *dikka*, a small platform on columns and with a kind of parapet. Beneath and in front of this was the desk which held a copy of the Koran, from which extracts were read during the prayers. At one point a *muballigh* would chant the equivalent of a hymn. Owen always liked the one about the spider showing favour to the Imam of Mecca by weaving its web in his cave.

When the worshippers protected themselves, bowing their head to the ground, Owen bowed likewise. Between prostrations he studied the people in the mosque – unobtrusively, of course, since it was forbidden to let your attention wander.

They were the usual mixture of Cairo rich and poor. In prayer all men were equal. A rich man or a man of rank might, however, bring his prayer mat with him.

At the last moment before the prayers began a man came into the mosque with a servant carrying a particularly beautiful prayer mat, which he placed on the ground for his master. When the prayers were over, the servant rolled up the mat and carried it out again behind his master.

The master was obviously a man of importance for as he left various people greeted him deferentially. A little group gathered around him and paused for a moment in conversation.

'It is good to see rich and poor pray together,' Owen said to the man beside him.

'It is,' agreed the man.

'Tell me,' said Owen, 'who is that worthy man?'

'It is the Pasha Ali Maher.'

Owen mingled with the worshippers as they came out into the sunshine. An unusual number of them seemed to be Sudanese.

There was no reason why they should not be. Cairo was a city of many nationalities – Greeks, Italians, all the shades of the Levant, Ethiopians – and each nationality had its own church. This one appeared to be for the Sudanese. There were a lot of Sudanese in Egypt, usually acting as servants. Not always though: there were well-to-do Sudanese as well, usually merchants of some kind, sometimes professionals. So the fact that there was an unusual density of Sudanese here was not especially striking. What was striking was that the Pasha Ali Maher was prominent among them.

Zeinab's father, Nuri Pasha, was not one of the most devout of Muslims. Even so, he had been to the mosque that morning. The mosque he had gone to was the El-Merdani, which, apart from being one of the most beautiful of Cairo mosques, and therefore pleasing to Nuri's highly developed aesthetic sensibility, was one of the most fashionable.

It was the one attended by the Court Pashas and also, since Court and Government went together, the one frequented by leading politicians. It was a place where Nuri could meet old cronies and also hope to meet new ones. It was a way of keeping in the swim – *au courant*, as the Francophile Nuri liked to put it. His influence these days was not, alas, what it had been: Nuri had been a minister once but then on an issue of importance had made the mistake of taking the wrong side – on this occasion, surprisingly, the British – and had therefore been eternally damned in Nationalist eyes. However, Court politician to the last, he still had hopes. So he made a point of cultivating the rising suns, and went regularly to the El-Merdani Mosque.

Owen, who knew his ways, fell in with him just as he was leaving.

'My dear boy!' cried Nuri. 'You're back!'

'Got in yesterday evening!' said Owen.

'Then you will certainly need a drink!' said Nuri, taking him by the arm. 'And I know just the one to give you! It is the Saint-Loup. Just in from Paris. It is a little strong for my taste – too much gin. Destroys the balance, I think. But, then, it comes from America!'

'It's new to me,' said Owen.

'But then you've been away,' said Nuri.

'Not *that* long!' said Owen.

'But in the south! A wasteland, dear boy. An absolute waste-land! Why do you let yourself be sent down there?'

'Interest.'

'Surely not! In the south?'

'A girl in a bride box,' said Owen. 'Perhaps you've heard?'

'I did hear something about it. It sounds intriguing. And sent to Ali Maher! Of all men!'

'Why of all men, Nuri?'

'He's a bit of a stick, you know.'

'I wanted to ask you about him.'

'Then we shall certainly need a drink. How about the Savoy?'

Owen wondered who was paying.

Nuri waved a hand. An *arabeah*, one of the horse-drawn cabs of Cairo, drew in.

The Savoy was not one of Owen's favourite hotels. It had a nice terrace, admittedly, although there was nothing that you could see from it except the traffic going across the Nile Bridge. The reception rooms, however, were cool and airy. As Nuri said, it was a pleasant place to hang around in – depending, of course, on who you wanted to hang around with. Nuri's tastes in that matter were not quite the same as Owen's.

They found a secluded alcove and prepared to sample the Saint-Loup.

'By the way,' said Nuri, 'I sent you a note . . .'

'And I sent it on,' said Owen, 'to someone who might be able to help.'

This was true, although less helpful than it seemed. Nuri Pasha seemed relieved, however.

'My dear boy!' he said, affectionately patting his hand, in the Arab way, on Owen's arm. The waiter, in full Arab robes, because this went down well with the tourists, of whom the Savoy was full, brought the two Saint-Loups in long glasses packed with ice, because, again, this went down well with tourists.

Nuri took a long sip. 'So, dear boy,' he said, putting the glass down, 'you wanted to know about Ali Maher?'

'Please,' said Owen.

Nuri took another sip and then looked at his glass

doubtfully. 'A strange fellow,' he said. 'His mother, they say, was a Sudani, although it is hard to be certain among all his father's wives. For some strange reason, certainly, he has always taken an interest in the Sudan. A taste for the savage, perhaps? He even took a wife from there himself. Although it worked out rather as you might expect. They had a boy, I gather, who wasn't quite right in the head.'

'I have met the boy.'

'That is more than most people have. His father keeps him out of sight. It might be awkward, you see, from the point of view of his political ambitions.'

'He has political ambitions?'

'Yes. He's trying to establish himself as a Unionist. You know, one of those fanciful fellows who works for the unity of the Nile Valley.'

'The union of the Sudan and Egypt?'

'A crackpot idea if ever there was one. But then, he's a bit of a crackpot himself. A century behind the times. The Sudan was part of Egypt seventy years ago. It was where we used to go to get our slaves,' said Nuri, with a tinge of regret.

He was thinking, perhaps, of Zeinab's mother, who had herself been a slave, although she had not come from the Sudan but from Middle Europe, another fruitful source of slaves to the Ottomans.

'And you say that his Unionist interests extend to practical politics.'

'He thinks they do. He thinks they could open a whole new area for Egyptian politics. "Dream on!" I told him. But the idea is not completely crazy. When I was young I occasionally thought along those lines myself. Occasionally. But then, of course, I grew up. I realized the British would never allow it.'

'But still he dreams?'

'An odd fellow, as I said. He lives in a sort of mental cocoon, cut off from the world around him, dreaming his dreams. He's always been like that. He comes from a good family but in his youth he seemed to go wild. He took off for the Sudan. The ancestral pull of the wild. Or just the influence of his mother. Anyway, he stayed there for some time. Went native. And when he came out he was a changed man. Began talking politics. Had seen the light. Been given a vision. Thought he could lead his people out of the wilderness. "Ali," I told him once, "you are not, believe me, another Mahdi!" He looked uncomfortable, and said: "Of course not!" But, you know, I rather fancy that he had that in his mind. Or some idea like that. Egypt and the Sudan joined together, perhaps, with him as its leader. Crackpot, as I say; but I think he takes the idea seriously.'

'He sees himself as Khedive?'

'I don't think that. Not any longer. It's more that he thinks if he makes enough noise, the Khedive will have to notice him and take him in.'

'Into the government?'

'I know! Crackpot! But not completely crackpot. His ideas start by being sane. But then, somehow or other, they go off the rails. Do you know what I think? I think it's in the family. That boy of his. Well, I think it's in him, too. In Ali Maher himself.'

# TWELVE

'It hasn't happened again, then?' said the Greek.

'Just the once,' said Nassir.

'That's a relief!' said Georgiades.

'I don't know,' said Nassir. 'She was some looker!'

'Yes, but, I mean, you wouldn't want to be spending all your time doing that.'

'I don't know,' said Nassir.

They both laughed.

'A married man like you!' said the Greek.

'Just because you're married, doesn't mean you don't notice,' said the clerk.

'The veil was made for men like you!'

'She wasn't wearing a veil.'

'She wasn't wearing a veil?'

'Not a real one. Just one of those half ones you see on posh ladies. And all filmy, so that you can half see through them.'

'I worry about you, Nassir!'

'You ought to be worrying about him!'

'Clarke Effendi?'

'Yes, Clarke Effendi. I never supposed he was like that.'

'Bowled over like that, you mean? Well, these quiet ones sometimes are, you know. They keep it shut in, and then suddenly it breaks out. Bang! Like that! Feel like it myself, sometimes.'

'Even with a wife like yours? It's you we should be worrying about!'

'I keep it bottled up.'

'Well, you surprise me, my friend. The things one learns when one gets to know people!'

'Oh, she's quite safe from me. But what about you, Nassir, will you be going along there now you know where she lives?'

'She's probably got a husband who's an all-in wrestler.'

'But you know where she lives?'

'In the Tisht-er-Rahal. Just off the Derb-el-Akhmar. Where it becomes the Sharia el Tabarneh.'

'By the Mardam Mosque?'

'That's right.'

'I know it well.'

He should. It was where Owen lived.

In his mail that morning Mahmoud received a letter. It was addressed to him personally at the Parquet.

It was from the Pasha's lady, who said that she was now in Cairo. She had brought Karim with her and they were staying at a small hotel called the Atbara near the Sukkariya Bazaar. It was a Sudanese name and the Sudanese Bazaar was nearby, on the other side of the Sukkariya. It was one of the poorer bazaars but there were some interesting shops specializing in the inlaying of mother of pearl and the general working of trocchee shells. Set against the dark wood usually used in Cairo they were very effective. Just beyond the end of the street was the famous mosque of El Azhar, which was also the great university.

Mahmoud turned the letter over in his hands. Why this sudden rush of letters from the Pasha's lady? And why to him?

He thought he could answer that one. He was probably the only member of the Parquet that she knew personally, and the Egyptian way was always to go through the personal.

But why was she writing to him anyway? Just to say she was in Cairo? Keeping him posted of her movement, as it were?

He kept coming back to his original answer: she wanted someone to know. And was afraid.

He made up his mind, took his fez, and got up.

As he approached the hotel, he saw, striding along the street ahead of him, the tall form of the Pasha Ali Maher. He dropped back. He didn't want to arrive there at the same time as the Pasha. In fact, he was having doubts now about going to the hotel at all. He held back uncertainly.

Suddenly he saw the Pasha's lady come out of the hotel, clutching Karim firmly by the arm. Karim, overawed by the number of people, the bustle and the traffic, kept tight to her.

She saw the Pasha and stopped.

Ali Maher went up to her. 'What are you doing?' Mahmoud could hear him from way down the street. 'Why have you brought that boy?'

'Why shouldn't I bring the boy? He is my son.'

'But here? Here! I told you never to bring him to Cairo again!'

'I didn't want to leave him.'

'It doesn't matter what you want. Those were my orders. That was the agreement,' he added more weakly.

'You broke the arrangement yourself. You told me to stay down there. And then, suddenly, you tell me to come up!'

'You, yes; but not the boy.'

'I was afraid to leave him.'

'Afraid?'

'Of you. And what you might have done to him if I had left him on his own.'

'Afraid of what I might do to him? He is my son!'

'I am glad you remember that!'

'Of course I remember that!'

'Only sometimes, I think you forget it.'

'I never forget it. It hangs on me like a great weight, all the time.'

'A weight you might want to get rid of.'

'Get rid of? Get *rid* of?' he shouted. 'He is my son! What are you saying? What are you saying, you terrible woman? What sort of a man do you think I am?'

'I think you are a man who has abandoned his son. You have no natural feeling. You lost that a long time ago. If you ever had any.'

'I did only what was best for him. You know that. If he had stayed in the city he would have been unhappy. You have seen him. He was not made for here. In the country he could be at ease with himself. There was nothing to bother him; there were no people who might trouble him. It was simpler for him. He could cope there. The city was too much for him.'

'You make him sound like a natural.'

'He *is* a natural! Treat him like one.'

'He is your son; treat him like one.'

'Why have you brought him here? Here, of all places?'

'I did not want him to be harmed.'

'Harmed?' He laughed bitterly. 'It is in the world that he is harmed. Out of it, when you were supposed to be keeping him safe, he would not be.'

She didn't say anything for a moment. Then she said: 'He is better. He is not what he was.'

'You deceive yourself,' he said.

'He is growing up.'

'But not as others do.'

'As others do!' she insisted. 'You have not seen him lately. You do not know . . .'

'I see him now.'

'He is bigger. And not unlike what you yourself were.'

'On the outside only.'

'There is growth inside, too,' she said softly. 'Where only a mother sees it.'

He shook his head.

'Take him home,' he said, not unkindly. 'He is better there.'

'When he stands beside you,' she said, 'many would not know the difference.'

'Would that were so!'

'It *is* so!' she insisted.

'You do not understand,' he said. 'There are people now who look to me. And if they come to him, not knowing, and find . . . that he is what he is, what will they think? Of me and all our plans?'

'You used to share those plans with me.'

'I would now. But it cannot be. Your duty is to him.'

'Is not your duty to him also?'

'Yes. But I cannot discharge it. I have other duties too.'

'Are they not less important?'

'No. They are wider than just you and me. As you know.'

'And so I have to bear those alone? By myself?'

'Yes.'

'It is hard.'

'I would not have it thus.'

'You used to speak to me gently.'

'And would again. God knows I do not like it thus. I had great hopes. *For* him as well as of him. But . . . they cannot be fulfilled. We have to accept that. But other hopes remain, and these may yet be realized. But they cannot be realized if he is here with me, where all can see him, and talk behind their hands. There is too much at stake. He must stay where he cannot be seen. And where he is happy.'

She looked down. 'He is less happy than he was.'

'Is there something wrong?' he said sharply.

'No, there is something right. He is growing up.'

He made a gesture of impatience.

'No,' she said. 'Hear me. He has needs. They are the needs of normal people, of every man . . .'

He was silent for a moment. Then he said: 'Cannot they be met? Cannot you find him someone? Some ordinary girl who would be glad of the money? Even if she would not do it at her father's command?'

'I have tried that.'

'There are always girls . . .'

'There was one he liked. He liked especially. I thought I could manage it. I brought them together. And he was happy, and I thought she was content. But she was not. She wanted more.'

'More?'

'Marriage.'

'Ridiculous!'

'That's what I said. And sent her away. But he pined. And in the end I had to bring her back. I still thought I could make it work, but . . . She was obstinate.'

'She refused?'

'Yes.'

'But did you not . . .? She was deaf to your commands?'

'Yes. But it cannot be quite like that these days . . .'

'Can it not? We shall see. Let me speak to her.'

'You will have her whipped.'

'She deserves it!'

'But still she may not be willing. And if you have her whipped, how will Karim take it?'

'Does it matter how he takes it? As long as he has her in the end.'

'It does matter,' she said. 'Although I do not quite know why it should. Things are different now. Or they are beginning to be different. Even in the village.'

'Money is still money. Even in the village. Why have you not spoken to her father? Let him do the whipping.'

'The father is weak. He will take the money, yes, and do the whipping. But still she will not obey.'

'Not obey! Then whip her some more!'

'It is not like that these days. And what will Karim say?'

'That is what you said before!'

'And I say it again: Karim has grown up. And, yes, it matters now.'

The Pasha was silent for a moment. Then he said: 'You have really messed this up!'

He stood there for some time, thinking. Then he seemed to make his mind up.

'We shall have to attend to this. But not now. I have other things to attend to. I wished to see you about something else.'

'Not Karim?'

'Not Karim. We had better go indoors.'

He led the way towards the hotel. The Pasha's lady followed obediently, together with Karim.

The Pasha halted at the door. 'Not Karim,' he said.

'What shall I do with him? I cannot leave him.'

'Let him stay here.'

'In the street? He will wander away.'

'God sustain us!' said the Pasha in exasperation.

'I will have to stay here with him.' The Pasha's lady shrugged. She was about to say something to Karim when she stopped. 'What am I to do with him?' she asked. 'I cannot let him wander about on his own. Not here, in Cairo, with the traffic.'

'You shouldn't have brought him,' said the Pasha.

'I thought you might want to see him.'

'Well, I don't.'

'Sometimes you seem to care for him,' said the Pasha's lady, 'and sometimes you don't.'

'I care for him,' said the Pasha impatiently. 'But there are times—'

'When you forget that you have a son.'

'I never forget that I have a son,' said the Pasha. 'Would that I could! I do not forget. But there are times when other things are more pressing. And this is one of them. I need to speak with you. Without the boy.'

'What am I to do with him?'

'How the hell do I know?' said the Pasha, boiling over. 'He shouldn't be here. You shouldn't have brought him!'

'But I *have* brought him,' said the Pasha's lady. 'What am I to do with him? While we talk?'

'Let him stay here.'

'I cannot talk to you in the street! Not about this!'

'You are talking already.'

'Not about . . . what I want to talk about.' The Pasha's lady considered. 'Very well,' she conceded, 'he can sit over there, in the square, and watch the trams. And we can talk over here.'

'Where everyone can hear us?'

'Where I can keep an eye on him.'

The Pasha gave in. 'Very good,' he said. 'Then send him over there.'

Karim had been hearing all of this and Mahmoud, watching from outside the carpet shop, where the rolls standing on end provided a screen, saw that he was troubled. He plucked continually at his mother's arm.

She stroked him gently on the cheek. 'It will be all right,' she said. 'I will not go away. I shall be watching all the time. You just go over there. See – there's a nice seat! Sit there and watch the trams. It won't be too long.'

Karim reluctantly obeyed.

'You shouldn't have brought him,' the Pasha repeated.

'What did you wish to see me about?'

'This mad prank of yours. Sending the body to me. In a chest.'

'It is a bride box,' said the Pasha's lady. 'I thought that appropriate.'

'I have told you: you are still my wife.'

'It is not that. The body is that of the girl Karim loved.'

'The girl Karim loved!'

'And that was her bride box. She brought it with her, thinking she was going to marry him.'

The Pasha seemed to be struck speechless.

'Now you can see why the box was appropriate,' said the Pasha's lady.

'What have you done?' cried the Pasha in anguish.

'I? I have done nothing. It is what you have done. And haven't done. That is important.'

'But the girl . . . How could you do something like this?'

'It had to be done. It was the only way. He would have gone on loving her otherwise. And she would never have surrendered him.'

'But . . .'

'It had to be. There was no other way.'

He seemed stunned.

'Down there,' she said, 'where there is so much space and the sky, and the sand, and that is all, you see things more clearly. You should come back. It would help you to see things clearly, too.'

'I wouldn't have seen them like this! What have you done, you terrible woman?'

'I have done what I had to do.'

'The police will track you down. And put you in prison. And then where will Karim be?'

'They are already knocking on the door,' said the Pasha's lady. 'The Parquet has already been.'

'But this is a disaster!'

'For Karim?' said the Pasha's lady. 'Or for you?'

The Pasha put his face in his hands.

The Pasha's lady regarded him for a moment with satisfaction.

'What is to be done?' he said hoarsely.

'It is not as bad as it seems,' said the Pasha's lady. 'And it is not quite as you think. You have always been ready to believe the worst of me. But it was not I who killed the girl.'

'Not you?'

'There are those who serve us loyally. They have an eye to what needs to be done. They are true to our family – yours, as well as mine. They could see that a marriage such as this would do great harm to the family. They decided it could not be.'

'My people, or yours?' asked the Pasha.

'Do not they serve us both?'

'Who?'

The lady did not reply. She stood there thinking. Once she looked across the square where Karim was watching the trams delightedly. 'One who wishes you well, and has always wished you and your family well.'

'He took it upon himself?'

The Pasha's lady nodded. 'I had sent the girl home. With her bride box. And on the way he must have decided that she should not come again.'

They remained talking for just a little longer. Once or twice the Pasha again put his head in his hands. If he had been the dominant one before, now it was she. He seemed to dwindle before Mahmoud's eyes. By the end he was almost in a state of collapse. The Pasha's lady, on the other hand, seemed to grow visibly. She dominated the exchanges now. Mahmoud could no longer hear what was said but rather thought that all of the lady's pent-up anger was being poured out on the Pasha's bowed head. He no longer spoke but listened in silence. At the end he drew himself up and almost tottered away.

The lady, perhaps weakened, too, found a seat and sat down by herself for a little while. Once or twice Karim looked back at her and she waved a hand to him. To show that all was well? Karim was clearly not sure. He kept looking at her and seemed to want to come over to her but then thought better of it and stayed where he was, watching the trams. A row broke out between two of the drivers. Both drivers descended from their trams and for a moment it looked as if they would come to blows. Such incidents were fairly common at Cairo's crowded streets and no one paid much attention. But the argument was sufficiently fierce as to draw Karim's attention and perhaps he forgot what had been troubling him before. His father now had gone away and his mother was sitting calmly by herself. Reassured, Karim concentrated on the trams.

Mahmoud wondered whether to carry on as he had intended and speak to the lady. He had read into her letter a possible plea for help. Now he was not so sure. She seemed able to look after herself pretty well. In the end his doubt was resolved for him by the lady catching sight of him and breaking into a welcoming smile. He walked across to her.

'How nice to see you!' she said, as if surprised.

'I got your letters,' said Mahmoud.

'Oh?'

It was as if they were of no interest to her now.

'Letters?' she said vaguely.

'Notes, rather. To say that you were coming to Cairo.'

'Oh?'

Again it was as if she had completely forgotten them.

Mahmoud decided that he had been reading too much into them.

'I hope you enjoy your trip to Cairo,' he said. 'And Karim, too.'

'Karim, yes,' said the Pasha's lady. 'It is a while since he was last in Cairo and he has forgotten. It is all very exciting for him. But also very confusing. In a little while he will begin to get headaches. A sort of migraine. Then I shall have to take him home.'

Mahmoud muttered something about medication.

The Pasha's lady smiled. 'You are a nice man, Mister el Zaki,' she said, patting him on the knee. 'And there are not many around.'

She stood up and Karim ran obediently back to her.

Later, he told Owen about it. Especially about the part concerning Suleiman.

'A cable came in this morning,' said Owen. 'They've picked up Suleiman and are sending him up to us.'

'To you?' asked Mahmoud. It was always a vexed question, this: who really ran the show in such circumstances? The Mamur Zapt or the Parquet? The British or the Egyptians? Usually both sides took care to see that it did not come to a head. The British deferred to the Egyptian authorities, so long as the authorities did what they were told.

Here, the issue was simpler than it usually was. Suleiman had been picked up in the Sudan, which meant that he had been picked up by the British. Egypt had no powers in the Sudan. Which was another thing that rankled.

'He will be repatriated back to Egypt,' said Owen carefully. 'And I imagine to the Parquet.'

He had better send a cable to make sure that this was so.

'Let me know how you get on with him,' he said. Mahmoud, bubbling up with pleasure, swore that he would. And, as a *quid pro quo*, passed on to Owen what he had learned from Idris. He had not really intended to do that, believing that the dealings of Idris's patrons were not a matter for the British. But in his delight he couldn't resist the temptation.

Owen's agents – different ones daily, so as not to arouse suspicions – kept continual watch on the warehouse and the madrassa. Nikos was busy tracking down who Ali Maher's political associates might be; and Georgiades shambled around, staying close to Nassir, and to Abdul, the porter, so as to be quite sure that they did not miss the moment when the arms were transferred to the madrassa. Nassir kept him informed about the dealings of his boss, Clarke Effendi, who seemed, however, to have dropped out of sight since he had returned to Cairo.

Suleiman duly arrived, under guard, at the Parquet, and Mahmoud went to interview him.

Suleiman, an assured, middle-aged Sudani from the Pasha's lady's family holdings on the coast, had been shaken by his unexpected arrest and then transfer to Cairo. He said nothing – was notably monosyllabic on everything, in fact – but his nervousness was betrayed by the constant switching of his eyes, as if fearing that a new attack could come from any quarter. He obviously recognized Mahmoud, although he had seen him only once, at the Pasha's lady's house, on that first day. Which made Mahmoud think that he had indeed been deliberately sent away.

'So, Suleiman,' he said easily, 'I catch up with you at last.'

Suleiman did not reply.

'Despite your being sent away so that I shouldn't.'

He waited, but again Suleiman made no response.

'So let me ask you now the question I would have asked if you had stayed with the others; it concerns Soraya's bride box.'

He waited, then went on: 'It was sent away, wasn't it? By the mistress, yes?'

'Yes,' said Suleiman, guardedly.

'Along with Soraya.'

'That is so,' Suleiman agreed.

'Were you sorry to see Soraya go? You were to be married to her, were you not?

'I was.'

'And then you weren't. How was that?'

Suleiman hesitated. 'The mistress wanted it otherwise.'

'Because Soraya was proving unsatisfactory?'

'Unsatisfactory, yes.'

'Did *you* find her unsatisfactory?'

Suleiman shrugged.

'She was to marry you. Surely she was satisfactory, then? Suleiman said nothing.

'To the mistress, perhaps, but not to you?'

'To neither of us.'

'Then . . .?'

'She would have it so.'

'But you didn't care for the girl?'

'She was forward. She would not have been a good wife.'

'To you. But perhaps to Karim?'

'She would have been a bad wife to Karim, too.'

'Why?'

Suleiman struggled for words. 'It would not have worked out,' he said.

'No? Why?'

'It was unseemly. She ought never to have thought of it.'

'Soraya, that is?'

'Soraya, yes. She was raising her eyes too high.'

'So the mistress sent her away. But, being compassionate, she had previously looked out another husband for her. You.'

'Me, yes.'

'But then she thought better.'

'Yes.'

'And sent her away. Back to her home.'

'Yes.'

'Did you go with her?'

Suleiman hesitated. 'Not I, no.'

'I was told you did. That you had command of her return?'

'No.'

'And saw to the bride box?'

There was a long delay before Suleiman responded. 'I saw that it was done,' he said at last.

'Did you not go with her?'

'I may have done. Part of the way.'

'But then returned?'

'Yes.'

'After having seen to her killing?'

'No. No. I did not do that.'

'But you had charge. Perhaps you merely said it should be done?'

'I did not see to it. Not that. The charge was passed to others.'

'Who?'

'I cannot remember.'

Mahmoud raised his eyebrows. 'The charge was passed to others? Whom you do not know?'

'That is so, yes.'

'A strange way of dealing with your mistress's charge! But perhaps she decreed that, too?'

Suleiman said nothing.

'Someone killed her, Suleiman. Either you, or someone you charged with the task. For she did not get home, did she? How was that?'

Suleiman's eyes began to look around. 'Perhaps bad men fell upon her,' he muttered.

'I think they did. But one of the bad men was you, Suleiman.'

'That is not so.'

'Then who? You were in charge, Suleiman. Which man was it?'

'I do not know. I do not know the men. They were bad men. They fell upon her.'

'Did you not stop them?'

'I could not stop them!'

'So what did you do?'

'I ran away.'

'There were men with you. Did they run away too?'

'Yes.'

'Who were these men who were with you? Were they men in the mistress's service?'

'Yes.'

'Their names!'

'I . . . I do not recall.'

'I shall ask, Suleiman. And let us hope that they say what you say. Or it will go ill with you. Now tell me another thing: when you got home, did you speak of this to anyone? Think carefully before you speak, because I shall ask them.'

'I . . . I did not speak of it to anyone.'

'Not even after so dreadful a thing?'

'I was afraid.'

'Did you not speak of this to your mistress? Surely she questioned you when you returned?'

'I spoke of it, yes.'

'She did not speak of it to me.'

'When I spoke of it, I spoke . . . generally,' said Suleiman, looking acutely miserable.

'Now tell me the truth,' said Mahmoud.

\* \* \*

It was Zeinab's turn to take the children to school that morning. Sometimes Musa took them and sometimes his wife; sometimes it was Aisha, Mahmoud's wife, and sometimes Zeinab. That morning it was Zeinab, which she quite liked. She would deposit the little girls at their kindergarten and then go on to call on friends – sometimes, indeed, Aisha – and occasionally to shop in the big French stores. Zeinab wasn't that interested in shopping but it was important for an emancipated Pasha's daughter to ensure that her turnout was *comme il faut* and in a dressy place like Cairo that required constant review.

The two little girls, Leila and Aisha's daughter Maryam, walked along hand in hand, chattering. Zeinab walked just behind them.

Somebody bumped into her, jostled her, in fact, and when Zeinab, taking umbrage, turned to address them, they spun away into the crowd.

When Zeinab turned forward again there were no longer two little girls but just one. Leila had vanished. A shocked Maryam, roughly thrust aside, her hand torn from Leila's, stood in mid-wail.

'Where is Leila?' said Zeinab, also shocked, and stunned by the suddenness of it all.

It took her a moment or two to realize that Leila had been snatched away.

Zeinab grabbed Maryam by her hand, then picked her up and carried her as that was easier, and began to hurry around asking people if they had seen a little girl, dark, being taken away. The crowd was sympathetic and soon everyone was looking.

'A little girl – Sudani!'

But Leila had disappeared.

A policeman was fetched. Others appeared, for Zeinab was not a Pasha's daughter for nothing, and threw her weight around.

When they didn't seem to be getting anywhere she commandeered an *arabeah* and went to the Bab-el-Khalk. The friendly McPhee, much agitated, had a dozen policemen in the street in a flash and, later, Garvin the Commandant added his reinforcement. In no time the streets were flooded with policemen.

But to no avail. Hours later they were forced to admit to themselves that little Leila had disappeared completely.

# THIRTEEN

Zeinab, who had never quite realized how much she cared for Leila, was distraught. Gradually, however, her distraction turned to anger. Mostly her anger was directed towards Owen. What was the point of having a Mamur Zapt for a partner if when it came to the crunch he was as powerless as you were? Zeinab had been close to power all her life, but now, when that power mattered most, it had all somehow dissipated.

She couldn't understand Owen's attitude. He seemed so calm. Garvin, McPhee, Nikos, even Georgiades, they all seemed so calm, whereas she was boiling, raging. It was, she decided, because they were cold. All Englishmen were cold. They had cold exteriors, unable or unwilling to display the slightest natural emotion, and they were cold inside. They didn't feel as Egyptians did. Nor as Arabs did, nor as any decent human being would. Cold, that's what they were: cold. She felt that Owen should be tearing around the place *doing* something; and yet all he did was sit silently in the house, before putting on his fez and going to his office, where, doubtless, he continued to sit silently, *doing nothing!*

She wanted to lash out, to hit someone. Why wasn't he doing that? The old Mamur Zapts they used to have under the Khedive would certainly have done that. They would have flogged someone. 'Why don't you do that?' she demanded.

'Certainly!' said Owen. 'But who?'

That irritated Zeinab even more and she stamped out of the room. Then stamped back in.

'Aren't you at least going to do *something*?'

Musa was doing something. He had found his old service rifle, loaded it, and gone grimly out on the streets. When he returned, briefly, to grab some food – his wife, who, knowing her husband, had it waiting for him – he went off again after having swallowed barely a mouthful, urged on by

Latifa, who afterwards went out and patrolled the streets herself. Of course it was useless, a complete waste of time. But at least they were doing something.

Zeinab wondered if she should go out, too, but had to admit, in her heart, that there was little point. McPhee had police out everywhere and if they couldn't find anything then it was unlikely that she would. And then Garvin pulled the police off the streets! Deciding it was a waste of time, probably. Another cold Englishman!

When Owen came home at the end of the day, she wouldn't speak to him.

Garvin had pulled the police off the streets at Owen's request. Even the far too gentle McPhee was appalled. He did not normally question decisions from above, but on this occasion, shaking with anger, he did. He went to see Garvin and Owen and was satisfied by neither.

In fact, there was method in the madness. The truth was that Owen and Garvin had bigger fish to fry.

On what had become his usual patrol now, Georgiades had run into Abdul, the porter.

'I'm hoping to have something for you soon!' he said to Abdul cheerfully.

'Not today,' said Abdul. 'I've got something else on.'

'Not . . .?'

Abdul nodded. 'Yes,' he said, 'I've got to get my men to the warehouse when the muezzin calls this evening.'

'Another night job?'

'It could be.'

'And you've no idea where? Keeping you in the dark as usual?'

'As usual. Except that Nassir says I'll know the place.'

'Oh, I see. Been there before.'

'And I'm not to say anything,' said Abdul. 'But *nothing*, says Nassir. And this time, he says, he means it. And Clarke Effendi will be standing over him and me and everyone else while we're doing it.'

Georgiades padded along to the warehouse.

'Can't stop to talk,' said Nassir.

'Not even for a cup of coffee?'

Nassir shook his head regretfully. 'The boss will be along at any moment,' he said.

Georgiades reported all this to Nikos, who had been expecting it for the last couple of days. A man had come to the madrassa the previous morning, gone in, but not to the teacher, and spent some time there. Then he had come out, and had been followed home by one of Owen's watchers. Home, it turned out, was the town house of the Pasha Ali Maher.

The police had been pulled off the streets so that their presence would not deter Ali Maher from any action that he was proposing to undertake. Guns, especially in that quantity, were important to the police. If they were linked to rioting, the situation would become very difficult to control.

They had to have priority. Both Owen and Garvin knew that. It wasn't just whatever unrest Ali Maher and his associates had in mind – that could be taken care of – but it was the possibility that it might spread that worried them. Shooting would invite return shooting and who knows where it would end?

So Owen waited in his office. He had made his arrangements and, for the moment, there was nothing more he could do. Reports came in continually through Nikos.

Reports came in, too, about the search for Leila. They were all negative. It was only too easy for anyone, especially a child, to disappear into the warren of little back streets that made up Cairo. You needed a lead. Without a lead he knew he would never find her.

He racked his brains all afternoon. Why had Leila been taken? Was it some crazy man who had taken a fancy to her? These things happened. They were not infrequent in Cairo. There was no wider rationality to them. They just happened, on a man's wild fancy. And so it was very hard to find a thread in them to follow.

Or was it something else? His mind went back to what Miss Skiff had said at the very beginning about the risk of Leila being snatched back by the slavers. Could that be what had happened? And yet it was a long way to come from Upper Egypt to do that. Was a single child worth it? Wouldn't a slaver have merely gone on to some other child, if numbers were that important? He would go to the length of coming up to Cairo only if there was something special about the child. What was so special about Leila?

And then, as he sat there, he realized what it was. His mind went back to Selim's reports on the conversation he had overheard in the temple at Denderah, the fears that Clarke had expressed about 'that child' hearing something. And seeing something, too. Him, and being able to recognize him.

Finally, he remembered what Georgiades had heard Clarke say at the Pont Limoun in Cairo. Again the fears of being recognized, of being implicated in the arms dealing. The fears must have run deep for he had recognized Leila at once, had known that she was the same child.

And the fears would have been reinforced, Owen now realized, by his own presence there at the caravan's encampment. For Owen now knew that the man who had stared at him so persistently that day had been Clarke. He had not known that at the time but Clarke had known him. The Mamur Zapt was not an unknown figure in Cairo. Far from it. Clarke had recognized him and must have wondered what he was doing in Denderah. And feared that it might be something to with him. In his mind it would all have been coming together.

And it was Owen himself who brought it together. The sight of him at Denderah would for Clarke have been a warning. And then that day at the Gare Pont Limoun the warning would have come home with force. It would have reinforced his anxieties about what Leila could reveal. And tipped Clarke into taking action.

It was Owen himself who had triggered the kidnap.

But at least he now knew that he had his lead. The lead that he had been looking so hard for.

Abdul and his porters came to the warehouse just as it was growing dark. Nassir was waiting for them and showed them in. A few moments later the tall, thin figure of Clarke slipped in after them. There was a brief delay and then the porters began to come out, two by two, each pair carrying a box between them. Last of all came Nassir and Clarke, watching over them as they made their way to the madrassa. Georgiades was watching, too, and he saw, a little later, the porters come out of the madrassa and go across the street with Nassir to be paid. Georgiades didn't need to go with them. He knew about this bit. Instead he waited beneath the columns of the madrassa and when Clarke came out, put his arms in a lock around his neck and waited for Owen's men to come up and take him away.

In his room at the Bab-el-Khalk Owen sat behind his desk. Opposite him, with his men standing over him, sat Clarke.

'There is one thing you can do,' said Owen, 'to make things easier for yourself. Tell me where the child is.'

Clarke started to deny all knowledge – but then looked at Owen's face and shrugged.

'For arms,' said Owen, 'you will receive a prison sentence. For the murder of a child, it will be worse.'

'Not murder,' said Clarke, shaking his head. 'I wouldn't do that.'

'No?'

'No. I haven't laid a finger on her.'

'I need to see her,' said Owen.

Clarke shrugged again. 'I have sent her away,' he said.

'To?'

'Denderah. The slaver's men will pick her up there.'

'And?'

'Take her to join the others.'

'If she comes to harm,' said Owen, 'it will be on your head, not just theirs. With the consequences I spoke of.'

Clarke hesitated, then looked at his watch. 'If you hurry,' he said, 'you can get there in time. The Pont Limoun. The train to Luxor leaves in forty minutes.'

Ali and Hussein were moving the bride box yet again. This time it was to go to the court house where the trial was to be held. The order had come late, after the normal working day had ended, and Ali and Hussein had questioned it. That had taken a satisfactory amount of time but had not resulted, as they had hoped, in the job being postponed until the next day. Indeed, they were doing it in the soft warmth of a Cairo evening.

They were just taking a shortcut through the precincts of the Pont Limoun when a girl's voice said: 'That's Soraya's box! What are you doing with it?'

'Why,' said Ali and Hussein, putting the bride box down, 'it's that little girl again!'

'Help! Help!' Leila cried.

'Shut up!' said the man holding her roughly by the arm. He tried to hustle her away.

'Help!' cried Leila again. 'He's a bad man, and he's stolen me! And I want to go back home. I want to go back to Zeinab!'

'Shut up!' said the man.

'Oh!' said Leila. 'He's hurting me!'

'Hey!' said Ali and Hussein. 'You can't do that!'

'Keep out of it!' said the man, showing them a knife.

'Help! Help!' shrieked Leila.

Others beside the two porters began to take notice.

'You let her go!' said Ali.

'She's a friend of ours!' said Hussein.

Leila tried to tear herself away from the man holding her. He cuffed her head and twisted her arm. Leila lowered her face and bit him.

The man swore and let go. Leila threw herself into the arms of Ali and Hussein.

The man was advancing on them with his knife when suddenly there was a sharp crack. The man fell forward over the bride box.

'Musa! Musa!' cried Leila.

Throughout the day people came and went at the madrassa, as they usually did. Some of them, as they left, were carrying packages, often rolls which might have been a prayer mat. These people were followed home by Owen's men. By the end of the day all the guns were gone. But Owen knew who had taken them and where they had gone to. So it was easy

that night to pick up both the people and the guns and
take them to the Bab-el-Khalk.

Last of all came the Pasha Ali Maher.

'Tell me,' said Owen, 'what the guns were for?'

'I don't know anything about any guns—' began the Pasha,
but Owen cut in.

'I know *who* they were for, of course, because they came
to the madrassa and collected them. Both guns and people are
now in my hands. But what were you going to do with them?
Start an uprising? Surely not. Even in the Sudan it wouldn't
get anywhere. It would be too small. And the British army
would be too big. And in Egypt you would get nowhere.'

'That is a matter of opinion—'

'Yes, I know. But it is not just my opinion. I have talked
to a number of leading politicians, and do you know what
their response was? They just laughed.'

'They would,' said Ali Maher bitterly.

'I know about your hopes to unite the Sudan and Egypt
politically. That is a perfectly sensible aim. Unlikely to succeed,
but not completely foolish. There are others who think like
you, both in the Sudan and in Egypt. But an armed uprising?'

Owen gently shook his head.

'That . . . that was not my intention,' said Ali Maher.

'No?'

'No. I knew there was no hope of getting anywhere with
that. My supporters are, as you say, not numerous, although
they are more numerous than you think. Of course I knew that
an armed insurrection was not likely to succeed. But that was
not my intention.'

He went on: 'I intended to organize demonstrations. A lot
of them. In the Sudan as well as in Egypt. Public demonstrations which would show the extent of the support there was
for the movement.'

'The movement?'

'In support of the great cause of uniting the Nile Valley
politically, so that it could speak with one voice.'

'Yours, of course.'

'I hoped that my voice would be heard, naturally. My voice
among others. I hoped that once I had demonstrated the extent

of my support the Khedive would feel compelled to take account of it and would call me into the Cabinet. With others, of course. It was not a case of supplanting the government but of augmenting it. I wanted to be taken seriously. To be able to shape the government's position. Change it.'

'In favour of unification?'

'Yes.'

'So why the arms? Cannot the arguments for your cause be put peacefully? In the normal political way?'

'They would not be listened to.'

'Oh, come! There are other politicians making the same points. You are not alone.'

'But we are not listened to as we would be if the arguments were backed up with guns.'

'Too small,' said Owen. 'Too few guns.'

'I know. But if there were a number of incidents, all over the place, in the Sudan as well as in Egypt . . .'

'You think it would create the illusion of numbers?'

'Not just the illusion. The reality. People would see and would come to hear more. And so the numbers would grow. They would become real. But without guns . . .' He made a gesture of dismissal. 'And demonstrations all over the place, Captain Owen? Would not you pay attention to that? Would not the Khedive?'

'Your defence is that you never meant to use the guns?'

Ali Maher looked down at his feet. 'We might well have used them. But sparingly.'

Owen laughed. 'In my experience,' he said, 'which is extensive, once these things start, they grow. You shoot at us, sparingly. We shoot back at you, sparingly. But it's not seen or felt as sparingly. And so the incident grows, and in the end no one is firing sparingly! Believe me, Pasha, when soldiers shoot, they do not shoot sparingly. The police might do so, perhaps, with someone standing over them. But soldiers! Believe me, Pasha. I was a soldier once. I know!'

To Ali Maher's surprise, coffee was brought in.

'This is unexpected, Mamur Zapt!'

'Now that there is to be no shooting, we can allow some

niceties. It does not, of course, affect the outcome. You will be sent for trial and you will be found guilty.'

'But punished accordingly?'

'It will be the Khedive who is punishing you, not the British.'

Ali Maher laughed. 'Preserving, as you say, the niceties. And, as you say, the outcome will be the same.'

'Yes. Actually, I wished to speak to you about something else.'

'Oh?'

'Karim.'

Ali Maher's face fell. 'Do not speak to me of Karim. Please!'

'I have to. We have to.'

'My family will take care of him.'

'Will they?'

'I shall tell them to. I have enough authority left to command in this.'

'And your wife – will she do as you tell her, with respect to Karim?'

Ali Maher frowned. 'She will have to.'

Owen shook his head. 'I don't see it,' he said.

'She will have to do as my family ordains.'

'But will she?'

Ali Maher did not reply for a moment. 'She is difficult, I know. Headstrong.'

'What if she doesn't do as they decree?'

Ali Maher made a little gesture of hopelessness. He was silent again for a moment, then declared: 'It is her fault. All her fault. If she had not given birth to a monster—'

'I don't think she has,' said Owen. 'Although to you it seems so.'

'The boy has his qualities,' Ali Maher conceded. 'But . . .'

'Would it not be best to leave him with her?'

'No!' said Ali Maher vehemently. 'She is not to be relied on. She is herself not right in the head. Look how she sent that girl to me!'

'Girl?'

'The one in the bride box.'

'Why did she do that?'

'To be revenged on me! For the failure of her own marriage.

Oh, I know her tricks! At heart she is still savage. This is one of her Sudani pranks. The bride box, don't you see? *Bride* box. And the dead girl inside. It was a sign. Oh, I know her signs. It was to tell me that all I did ended in death.'

'*She* sent the box to you? With Soraya inside?'

'Of course!'

'Not Suleiman?'

'Suleiman only did her bidding.'

'He was *that* faithful a servant to her?'

'He is from her tribe. From her family. So he would do as she required. Now do you see why I cannot leave Karim with her? If I am in prison, what might she do to the boy? She loves him, yes, but it is a mad love. It is sometimes like that with these woman who bear monsters. Their love is all the fiercer because they have brought forth a monster. How can I hand him over to her?'

'But you did hand him over to her!'

'I was a fool. I thought that while I was there in the background I could watch over him from afar. I couldn't bring myself to be closer. I had wanted a boy so much. And then to find . . . this! So I had to put him away. And she seemed to love him – she *did* love him! So I thought it best . . . But now to have *this* . . . this crazed prank! Her mind has gone, it must have! How can I hand the boy over to someone like her?'

'You are a faithful servant of the lady,' said Owen.

'I hope so,' said Suleiman.

'Even though she sometimes asks hard things of you?'

Suleiman looked startled. 'Yes,' he said. 'That is so.'

'Take the boy, for instance. Karim. She expected your help with him.'

'And rightly so. Was he not my mistress's son?'

'Nevertheless, afflicted as he was, it cannot always have been easy.'

Suleiman shrugged. 'In my country,' he said, 'it is the custom to treat the afflicted as one of the family.'

'The family, then, was yours, as well as hers. And his?'

'That is so, yes. That is how we see it.'

'When he was a child it was easy. Easy still, although

growing more difficult, when he was a youth. But when he grew to manhood, and began to feel manly needs, then it became very difficult.'

'That is so, yes.'

'For her – and perhaps for you?'

Suleiman did not reply.

'Especially when Soraya came into the household.'

'That girl was a trouble maker!'

'She answered to Karim's needs, though. And all might have been well, had she been content.'

'She was treated well. Too well, in my opinion. It made her forget who she was.'

'And she raised her eyes too far.'

'Too far, yes,' agreed Suleiman.

'So what was to be done?'

'The lady sent her away – rightly so.'

'But it did not work out.'

'It should have worked out,' said Suleiman. 'It was the right thing to do.'

'And the wrong thing to bring her back?'

'The wrong thing, yes. The boy pined, and the mother's heart was torn.'

'And Soraya had brought her bride box.'

'She should have been sent away immediately!'

'But she was not. Until it became too late.'

Suleiman said nothing.

'Something had to be done,' said Owen. 'Did the idea come from her or from you?'

Suleiman just shook his head.

'I don't think it would have come from you,' said Owen. 'It was not your place. You merely did – faithfully – as you were told.'

There was a long pause, and then Suleiman said, 'I do not know how it came about.'

'Soraya was sent home again. Her bride box, too. You were charged with seeing to it.'

Suleiman did not speak but inclined his head.

'But Soraya never got home.'

'Men fell upon her.'

'So you say. But no men have been found. The men who were carrying the bride box were sent away. Leaving you, Suleiman.'

Suleiman bowed his head again. 'I must answer for it,' he said.

'You must certainly answer for what you did. But is it right that you alone should be blamed?'

Suleiman looked at him.

'When you were merely being faithful.'

Suleiman was silent for a long time. Then he said: 'It is my place to be faithful.'

'And there was much to be faithful to. The family, for instance: what was best for the family? And you could not leave out the master's family. Duties are owed there, too. And there, it seemed, the duty was clearer. The master's family was a great one. There might be a place for Karim in it. But not for Karim and *his* son, if son there should be. Lest the son should be like him. Was that how it was reasoned?'

'It may have been.'

'Or perhaps it did not even need to be reasoned. It just had to be understood. And someone like you, Suleiman, who had been in the family for a long time, understood that very well.'

'It may have been so.'

'The lady did not need to spell it out. Perhaps she did not even need to speak. You knew what was expected of you, and, as a faithful servant, you carried it out.'

'It may have been so.'

'*Did* she speak of it?'

Again there was a long pause.

'Perhaps,' said Suleiman. 'But I do not recall.'

Mahmoud received a letter from his friend Idris. It was post-marked Suakin, Sudan. The 'Sudan' was heavily underlined by Idris and there was a big examination mark beside it.

*Dear Mahmoud,*
*As you will see from the postmark, I am in one of the outer rings of hell, recognizable by the heat. It is much, much hotter than even Upper Egypt. My brains are fried*

*to a cinder. My sap is dried up. Beneath this huge open sky, with nothing between me and the sun, I shrivel.*

*The heat! The flies! The stink of trocchee shells on the beach when I go there in search of air! The lack of anyone to talk to.*

*And so I talk to you, or, at any rate, write to you. Do please write back to me, so that I will know that there is life beyond the grave! At the moment, as I dwindle, I fear that everything outside me dwindles. Hopes, ambitions, ideals are the first to shrink.*

*As you see from the postmark – and, yes, they do have a post office, where the pilgrims go to get their documents stamped and everyone else to pay their taxes – I am in Suakin, the City of the Dead, as they so rightly call it. Once it was a big, thriving city, the main port on the coast, through which all the pilgrims passed on their way to Mecca, but the ships got bigger and the water needed to be deeper, and so the whole city had to move further up the coast and became Port Sudan. The houses now are empty. Only the mosquitoes and the flies now wing their way through the deserted streets. Only the occasional stray dog searching for offal. And behind the dog, me.*

*Life has migrated, Mahmoud, and I alone am left to handle my master's business. The taint of trocchee shells lies heavily upon me. The true smell of business!*

*This place is backward beyond belief. Only today I heard that a slaver was expected in the town. Yes, like that, a slaver! Expected! I thought that sort of thing had died out years ago. And now . . . expected! Part of the natural scheme of things. Taken for granted.*

*While you and I and fools like us work for the improvement of our country and believe that through our reforms we can make the world a better place! No, Mahmoud, it is not so. Here in the desert everything runs away into the sand. We achieve nothing. Evil goes on, as it has gone on for centuries. They tell me that many of the slaves are children, sold by their families, or kidnapped from their families. And much desired by the wealthy families of the Saudi peninsula. And perhaps they will be better off with them than where they are. Only it sticks in my gullet, Mahmoud. I don't like it. This is not a world that I can believe in or accept.*

*I thought it belonged to the past but tomorrow the slaver will come in with his caravan, quite openly, and settle down in the market-place to await the ship. No wonder the place stinks!*

*I know that if I stay here I shall stink, too. And so, sooner or later, I shall come back to you, Mahmoud, all smelly but with a tiny part of my integrity intact.*

*Write to me, Mahmoud, before I slip away into the sand, too, and become just a mirage, floating in the air, quivering, just another bad smell in the stale air.*

# FOURTEEN

F ish teemed in the tepid water, fish of all sizes and colours. There were pink fish, crimson fish, yellow fish, green, fish white and fish black. There was one striped white and black in rings like a bull's eye. They nudged at the fallen stonework of the jetty, slid silently through the shadows, rose sometimes to sparkle in the sun.

At the end of the causeway, as tall as the minaret of the adjacent mosque, was the Wakkala, once the glory of the port, its largest warehouse, then a *caravanserai* into which camels brought loads of cotton, ivory, gum, senna leaves and melon seeds.

And slaves, of course, although these had walked behind the camels on their way to the Wakkala where they would await the boats that would take them across the Red Sea to the great slave markets of the Middle East.

It was to the Wakkala that Abdulla, the slaver, had brought the slaves he had collected. They had arrived the night before, in not too bad shape, his informants had told Macfarlane, of the Sudan Slave Bureau, who had had the caravan watched from the moment it had crossed the border from Egypt into the Sudan.

He had had time to cable Owen and ask him if he wanted to be in at the kill. Owen had said that he did. He had his own reasons for wanting to talk to Abdulla.

He had taken the train down to Luxor and then on to Atbara, the big railway junction in the Sudan, and then another train, the old troop carrying one, on to Port Sudan, a camel's ride from Suakin. He had reached the Dead City just before dawn and walked along the sea front, admiring the fishes, to the Muhafaza, about the only building still working in the deserted city. The Muhafaza was the old post office and the ottoman half-moon was still carved above its front door.

It was where Idris, Mahmoud's friend, now spent most of his time.

This was where Owen was to meet Macfarlane and the Camel Corps soldiers he had brought with him. They had arrived during the night and now stood beside their camels outside the Muhafaza.

'All right,' said Macfarlane. 'Shall we proceed?'

The soldiers began to slip silently through the empty streets. Everything was dark and quiet. A few doors hung half open in the street and the occasional *mashrabiya* window – still beautiful, though lined now with sand and dust – leaned out above. As the sun rose and began to reach the streets there was sometimes a flash of blue as it caught one of the old plates embedded in the mud brick of the walls. The old builders had used anything there was to hand and that included the plates brought over the sea from China by the seafaring Muslim sailors.

The soldiers stopped and then moved forward more cautiously. A whistle blew and the soldiers burst into the large courtyard of the Wakkala. The few men there looked up in shock.

Over in one corner a group of children, huddled together against the wall, turned towards the soldiers, amazed.

A tall Arab came out of one of the buildings. Macfarlane went up to him.

'Greetings, Abdulla!' he said. 'I see you're still at it.'

The children would go back to Atbara and then Khartoum by train, where arrangements would be made to reunite them with their parents. Abdulla would be going to Khartoum, too, only with the Camel Corps soldiers.

But first, Owen wanted to have a talk with him.

'Slaving is one thing,' said Owen. 'Murder is another.'

'Murder?' said Abdulla.

'Do you not remember Soraya?'

Abdulla shook his head. 'I had nothing to do with that,' he said.

'Did you not speak with her father?'

'Yes, but . . .'

'You tricked him. You spun a web with fine words.'

'He was willing to be tricked,' said Abdulla.

'What did you tell him?'

Abdulla spread his hands. 'That a fine future awaited her. If she played her cards right.'

'Not so fine,' said Owen.

'It could have been fine,' Abdulla insisted. 'It was a worthy household. And she was well pleased.'

'Tell me,' said Owen, 'why did you go to that house? Why did you seek her out?'

'I was asked to.'

'By the lady?'

'By the lady, yes. She had her own designs.'

'Which included you. She knew you of old. You come from her parts. Are you one of her family?'

'Distantly, yes. I was never close.'

'But close enough for her to call on you when she wanted something done.'

'Close enough, yes. And all she wanted was that I should seek Soraya's family out and speak to the father.'

'And tempt him, yes?'

Abdulla shrugged. 'He was willing to be tempted.'

'You succeeded, as she went to the lady's household. With her bride box?'

'No, no, that was the second time.'

'Since you had succeeded with your honeyed words the first time, she went to you again.'

Abdulla shrugged once more. 'I happened to be in those parts.'

'And again you succeeded. And this time she took her bride box with her. Did you suggest that? Was that part of the web you span?'

'It was her father's doing. He wanted to believe and so he believed.'

'You did not put him straight?'

'Why should I put him straight? The chance was there for her to take.'

'What she wanted was not what the lady wanted.'

'That is no concern of mine.'

'Your job was merely to spin the web and trap the fly. What

happened to the fly afterwards was not, as you say, your concern.'

'So,' said the Pasha's lady, looking around her curiously, 'you have made . . . what is it that the English say? My husband would tell me, but he, alas, cannot be here. "A clean sweep"? Is that the expression? My husband is in prison awaiting trial; the slaver is in some dark hole in Khartoum; and Soraya's killer is in some slightly less dark cell here in Cairo.'

'Not quite,' said Owen. They were in his office at the Bab-el-Khalk. He had asked the lady to come and see him before she returned to the estate at Denderah.

'Not quite? What, then, remains? Are you going to put the rest of us in prison, too?'

'Perhaps,' said Owen.

A phrase of Shakespeare's was running through his mind: 'All are guilty, all.' In a traditional society – such as the one, perhaps, about which Shakespeare was writing, and Lear was talking – individual responsibility was diffuse. An individual could hardly ever be taken by himself. He could not be separated from social bonds – the bonds of family, clan, tribe, religion. They all imposed their demands on him. And, conversely, he or she could impose demands on them. Where did responsibility begin and end? With the nexus of which he or she was part? Or with the individual?

'Perhaps?' the lady repeated, shaken.

'I was thinking of Soraya.'

'But surely there is no "perhaps" about that? Suleiman killed her and has confessed!'

'Not quite confessed.'

'But, surely . . .'

'He has not denied it. There would be no point. He killed her, all right. But does he see himself as fully responsible? I don't think he does. He sees himself more as an agent. Of someone else. Of other people behind him, and of other forces and demands.'

'He had accomplices?'

'No. If anything, he was the accomplice. Soraya had been

trapped in a web. But the web was spun by someone other than Suleiman.'

'We are all caught in webs,' said the Pasha's lady.

'But some of them are of our own making.'

'What are you saying?' she demanded.

'Both Soraya and Suleiman were caught in a web. But the web was spun by you.'

The lady stood up to go. 'These are things easily said,' she said.

'But not easily proved in a court of law, I know,' said Owen. 'Actually, a Muslim court would weigh these things better than an English court. It weighs the influences that had been brought to bear upon an individual, too, before guilt is assigned. And the loyalties that they are obliged to adhere to.'

'How unfortunate, then,' said the Pasha's lady, as she turned to go, 'that, if you are right, and if I quite grasp what you mean, Suleiman would be tried by an English court.'

Owen rose to show her out. 'I think you should return to Denderah, lady, with your son. And stay there. And in future take heed of the strings.'

'Strings?'

'The strings that you pull. Lest the consequence affect others than you intend.'

'I know,' said the Pasha's lady, laughing merrily. 'I have just thought of another English expression: lest chickens come home to roost!'

'Bear in mind, lady, that if they did, the person affected might be Karim.'

The lady stopped. 'How so?'

'Your husband does not think you are a fit person to be entrusted with his son. If you were removed from the scene, lady, Karim would be handed over to his family. Take heed in future, lady, of the things you do. Or I will see that what he wants comes to pass.'

A few days later Owen had risen even earlier than usual and was standing on the rooftop of his house, looking down at the nearby public gardens, where the birds were just beginning to stir, and at the Nile curling away beyond them. A solitary felucca was skimming around the bend and from nowhere he could hear the shouts of workmen, perhaps out with the water carts. Already the sun was hot enough for wreaths of vapour to start rising from the water. But here on the rooftop it was cold enough for him to put on his dressing gown. In one of the pockets his hand found a trocchee shell, the one that had been with Soraya when she died.

He thought about Soraya. He was still not sure that he had done the right thing about the Pasha's lady. Why should the rich walk free while the poor, who may merely have been doing their bidding, pay the price which really their masters, or mistresses, should have been paying?

There had been the problem of coming down firm on one person's responsibility where responsibility was diffused and spread among many. There had been the needs of Karim. Egypt was a society sympathetic towards the afflicted and the Pasha's family would not treat Karim harshly.

But that was not the same as a mother's love, even if the love was unbalanced and excessive. Karim would be better off with his mother. All the same, Owen was not altogether happy about the way he had caused things to work out. Perhaps he was becoming too preoccupied these days with parental issues. Lately Zeinab had been spending a lot of time with Aisha and there had been much putting of heads together.

There was the issue of what to do with Leila, too. There was no question of returning her to her father. He would not, in any case, be in a position to support her for quite some time. So what then? Should she stay with them in the house? But there was really no reason why she should now. There was no longer any fear that the slaver might snatch her back. Zeinab, it is true, would miss her if she went. But Zeinab might have other things on her mind soon.

Fortunately, Musa and Latifa had come up with a suggestion: Leila could stay with them. Their own children had grown up and, as Latifa said, the house felt empty. Leila already looked on them as her parents and would be more than happy. And, as Zeinab said, they would not be far away.

Leila, actually, was not far away now. In fact, she had come

up on to the roof, as she often did these mornings, and was
playing with the wooden giraffe that Owen had brought home
for her from the Sudan. Zeinab had put a sand tray up there,
and Latifa had found a carrot top whose leafy fringe made it
a shady palm tree, and the giraffe roamed happily round the
sand tray and even out across to Owen on the roof. No, even
Miss Skiff would accept that there was no longer any need to
worry about Leila.

Soraya, though . . . Owen was still wondering if he had
done the right thing. He thought he would go and talk with
Mahmoud about it again. When they had talked before,
Mahmoud had stood out strongly for the judicial process. But
then, unexpectedly, Aisha had butted in. Could Mahmoud not
think less about laws and more about people, she demanded?
Karim, as every parent knew (said rather pointedly) would be
better off with his mother, and she would be better off with
him. Mahmoud and Owen had both protested, before Zeinab
had asked hadn't the decision already been made? Why were
they still going on about it?

They might go on about it some more that evening, thought
Owen, who was still not satisfied and knew that Mahmoud
was having lunch that afternoon with his friend Idris, who had
just returned from the Sudan. Like Mahmoud, Idris was an
idealist and a reformer and would certainly have ideas about
the balance to be struck between justice and mercy. Idris would
probably have ideas, too, since he had just been in the Sudan,
of balances to be struck between traditional justice and
Mahmoud's modern suggestions. Although, according to
Mahmoud, Idris was less keen than he had been on putting
the world to rights.

Down on the river there was the splash of an oar. A funny
little boat was pulling out to ferry some people to the other
side. Why couldn't they just walk over the bridge? he wondered.
But he could see that also in the boat were hens running loose,
chicks in a hamper, an old woman with about ten baskets, two
small boys and a very, very old man who probably couldn't
walk very far, and Owen thought that occasionally there was
still something to be said for the old ways.